DEDICATION

This one is for all the fans! Be sure to sign up for my mailing list at *lolafaust.com*!

-L.

CONTENTS

PREFACE

I finally finished the story. Here it is, in all its sex-soaked saurian splendor.

Thanks to Katee Robert, doyenne of demon romance, for inspiration! And to all my sensitivity readers, who, after being revived with smelling salts, suggested the following trigger warnings:

TRIGGERS:

Dinosaurs, sex, dinosaur sex, ornithoscelidaphobia, fisting, vore, gore, pain, blood, sadism, masochism, captivity, camping, cults, candy, insects, arm trauma, shoulder trauma, amputation, interspecies sex, menstruation, brains, carnivorism, sexism, misogyny, speciesism, classism, ableism, abusive parent, abusive coworker, infidelity, pornography, fire, water, forests, farms (working and dormant), unorthodox use of personal lubricant, implicit and explicit threat of sexual assault, inaccurate dinosaur anatomy (for the sake of the story), accurate dinosaur anatomy (for the sake of accuracy), feathers, Canada, South Dakota, Wal-Mart, cornfields, cow-tipping, barns, pickup trucks, threat of police violence, guns, gunshot wounds, immigration paperwork, portable toilets, decapitation, taffy-pulling, animal slaughter, religion, PTSD, venture capital, vegetables.

Thanks also to the lovely #booktok community on TikTok, particularly Ryann Rice and Bailey Chadwick, for all the great videos and the support. And thanks to Devendra Banhart, unironically one of my favourite musicians, for the shoutout in *GQ*.

No matter what you get out of reading *Wet Hot Allosaurus Summer*, I hope you enjoy it. Thoroughly.

You can find all of my books on Amazon, or via LolaFaust.com, where you can also get in touch with me! I don't bite, I promise.

Unlike Big Al.

Wet Hot Allosaurus Summer

CHAPTER ONE

Tanis climbed onto the biggest barn to watch the dinosaurs. Her whole body hurt from a grueling day of ranching. There was dirt under her chipped nails, and a big brown stain on her blue jeans from where she'd fallen in the mud while milking Dusty, her favourite heifer. In the fields, the cows mooed contentedly, chewing clover. The evening was thick with pollen and the warm buzz of bees and chirping crickets.

Tanis' body was tight and lean from seventeen years of working alongside her father and brothers on their farm. Had she grown up in the city around men who were not her family, she might've known she was beautiful. She'd inherited her mother's generous breasts and backside, but hard labour had crystallized her curves, made them more severe and striking. Though Tanis knew nothing of her own beauty, she knew of the beauty of the dinosaurs, whom she watched every night without fail.

"Astonishing," the news had proclaimed, so many decades earlier, "that they should live among us, recreated out of DNA collected from rocks." The first generation lived as zoo animals. They might have remained sideshow attractions, but a biologist at the Chicago Centre for Paleolithic Genetic Research noticed the way Albertosaurus and Allosaurus would work in groups to systematically smash rocks. Multinational conglomerates funded a bold dinosaurs-to-work experiment. It succeeded beyond their imagining. And thus, like so many other species, dinosaurs were at last belatedly domesticated and integrated into the workforce of man.

They proved especially good at raw material extraction: they thrived when introduced into the tar sands, iridescent beasts growing warm and strong by the rainbow-slicked pools of crude. They were primordial beasts, drawn always back to the slick and pumping heart of the earth.

Tanis had grown up on these histories and they seemed like myths to her. She couldn't imagine a time before dinosaurs were everywhere, a time when people protested by bombing research centers and zoos. It seemed to her as stupid as shooting at cows.

Her family lived in the foothills on some of the last remaining farmland in Alberta. From the roof of the biggest barn, she could watch the extractions, see the bodies of the pterodactyls, as perfectly engineered as airplanes but of warm flesh. During the day, the hordes of Tyrannosaurs and smaller carnivores were visible. Sometimes a raptor would scamper through their fields, scaring the cows. She sketched them in secret sometimes, their long necks, blues and greens. Learning how to draw their feathers was hard at first, but eventually became her favorite part. She loved how the scales and feathers worked together for heat maintenance and protection. When her father found her sketchbook, he slapped her across the face.

"Those ugly lizards are going to dig our graves," he growled.

Tanis learned to keep the sketchbook under her pillow when she slept and carried it in her knapsack across the farm during the day. Each night she dreamed she'd wake up as a giant and beautiful dinosaur and that she would flee her small life as a farm girl.

The sun pulled the shadows of trees and oil rigs long across the fields. Tanis closed the sketchbook and set it on the shingles. A clover-sweet breeze tugged strands of honey hair out of her ponytail. She pulled her flannel across her chest. Her nipples prickled with the evening coldness. In this light, the dinosaurs were perfect. They shone deep amber and crimson. That colour made her heart rush.

Every day, they seemed closer. The farmland was shrinking, true, but it was more than that. She felt like she could throw a stone and hit one. She dug in the gutters of the barn and grasped a flat rock. The stone arced through the clean air and landed a few feet from the barn, nowhere near the working dinosaurs. She threw another, so hard she thought her shoulder might pop out of its socket. She threw another and another until the gutters by her feet were empty and her arm hurt. At last it was dark and Tanis felt cold and alone.

Her body knew the barn—every foothold and loose corner of siding—and she slid quickly down its face. The first thing she noticed when she landed was an unusual smell. Like fish, she thought, and flowers, but not unpleasant. Perhaps her mother was experimenting for dinner. Tanis heard a hiss and watched her cat Misty—a grey Persian—scatter into a hole in the barn. Then she saw the leg.

It took Tanis a second to realize what she was looking at. The dark iridescent feathers shone in so many colours she would never be able to render them, even if she spent her whole life drawing them. She followed the tree-thick leg up to its strong hips, wide chest and, finally, the glorious saurian head, eight feet above the barn floor. The word came unbidden into her mind: Allosaurus. His eyes were the deep green of oceans she had only imagined in her dreams. His cheekbones looked carved from prehistoric cliffs. His feather 'do was coiffed in a sexy and hip honky-tonk curl.

He let out a low and deep roar like a tractor coming on after a long winter. His body reminded her of a living lake, the way one move would ripple across his feathers. He reached out. She saw his communication device, the wires wound into his claw. After some violent misunderstandings, all infant dinosaurs were now hardwired with a bioelectric communication device that allowed them to speak telepathically with their human foremen. She knew with one touch she would be able to see into his mind and he would be able to see into hers.

She backed away, fearful of… of what? She should have felt instinctive terror at the giant predator's presence, but it wasn't that at all. Was it something else? Was it fear of really communicating with him, of knowing what he was thinking—did he feel the same way? He stared into her with such a begging look…

She let him touch her temple and felt the quick zing of their minds tuning into the same channel.

I've watched you, too, Tanis, his mind said into her mind. Then he backed away. He was shy, too. He stared down at his claw feet.

Half afraid and half wanting, Tanis let him sniff her neck. His mouth parted and she saw his rows of razor teeth. His breath smelled hot and earthy, like a barbecue. She couldn't distinguish fear from desire. Goosebumps prickled over every inch of her soft human skin. He touched her temple again with his talon and she watched his fantasy like a movie projected into her skull—he didn't know whether to eat her or take her from behind and make her his mate.

His tongue slid out of his mouth and brushed her behind the ear with unexpected softness. The feeling bloomed all down her spine. She felt a wetness between her legs, something she'd only experienced once or twice while horseback riding. It made her throb.

He licked her again. This time, harder, more ardently down her entire neck, tasting her fear and sweat. His tongue was as big as her whole hand. She imagined other places he could lick her with it. She reached down and gently stroked the feathers of his chest, muscled from labour. His skin was hard like a leather saddle, but his feathers felt like tulip petals, soft and slightly wet. She began exploring him with her hands.

"Tanis, move!" She heard her father shout from behind her. She saw him, short and stocky, sickly human, with a pipe sticking out of the corner of his mouth, shotgun cocked.

"No," she shouted, and leapt in front of the Allosaurus.

The shot boomed through her eardrums and into her shoulder. It sent her flying through the air like a sack of flour. She landed on a hay bale, coughing, wind knocked out of her. The magic of the encounter was gone. She felt cold and shattered, blood gushing from her shoulder, soaking her flannel shirt.

The dinosaur hissed and wailed, lunging at her

father. He was several times larger than the man. She sensed his hot fury. He was upon him in seconds, teeth out.

"No," Tanis shouted.

The beast turned back, eyes narrowed at her. Though they were not connected by his telepathy device, Tanis could feel his thoughts.

You would save him?

Tanis nodded sadly. As much as she had hated her human life, she'd lived with her father for seventeen years and felt some sympathy for him: his small life and hatred. The dinosaur forgot her cowering father and returned to her. He lifted her in his talons with a remarkable tenderness and held her to him. She smelled the fish and flower scent that had first identified him and it made her feel safe. She held on tight as he ran with her, springing on quick lizard legs out of their barn and across their property. All of the stars in the sky swirled as they ran together as one creature.

Behind them, her father and brothers had assembled, all with shotguns, firing. But Tanis and her mate were sprinting too quickly; the gunshots came nowhere near the fleeing couple.

After an age of running, the blasts grew qui-

22

et and impotent. She saw her brothers and father fade into even tinier specks. She thought her heart would burst as she curled into the warm and welcoming shoulder of her new love, the love she had observed unnoticed for so long. Was it shock or blood loss or just dawning realization? Her old life was over.

Finally all the senseless noise from her farm had disappeared. It was dark. The dinosaur stopped running and set her down in the field. The cold air rushed around her.

Pain burned in her shoulder. He touched her forehead.

What do I call you, she asked.

We don't really have names, he said, but you can call me Big Al.

She repeated the name out loud and telepathically. Big Al. It was so beautiful to her. So simple. She couldn't believe she was here in the field with a dinosaur, her dinosaur, Big Al. He rubbed his muzzle all over her body. Again her skin perked up. She didn't know she could feel this way—like she was jumping into a freezing lake while being burned alive. Big Al popped her buttons easily with his talons. He tore off her pants like they were made of paper. Tanis had never been naked in front of a man before, never mind a man dinosaur. She tried covering herself with her uninjured arm, but he pinned it against the cold earth and, with one fluid motion, ran his tongue from her injured shoulder down to her hip.

Tanis gasped. He slid his tongue back up her body with extreme tenderness, like a hot summer breeze. With the tip, he drew circles on her neck, working his way from the base of her ear to her collarbones. His every touch made her tingle. He traced her breasts, circling her nipples, which leapt up. They hardened with a pleasure that was almost painful. Big Al continued down her body, licking her belly and inner thighs. He kissed her ankles. With his strong jaw he pushed apart her legs. Her thighs quivered. He licked her ardently, like she was the most delicious thing in the entire world. Tanis felt her whole body melt. He grasped her butt with his talons, tasting her deeper and deeper.

Pleasure moved through her in waves, rippling.

With his tail, he grabbed her around the waist and lifted her up so that she was face to face with him. He held her to his chest. She could feel his warmth and his power, his love emanating. He lowered her onto his sex. She felt it, massive, rubbing against her own warm wetness. He slid her up and down along it, wetting himself. Then he entered her. His talons dug into her shoulders, forcing her down, to accept all of him inside of her. She felt like she was going to be torn apart, from his size and also from the intensity of her own pleasure. He pushed deeper.

Everything about him was too much. Tanis could barely breathe. She saw colours—the bright reds and ambers of dinosaurs flying at twilight. There were stars behind them, burning hot, swirling in her eyelids. Pain gave way to pleasure. She cried quietly at first and then louder, letting out big wet wails timed to his every movement. He was churning her insides into a soft satisfying butter. She gripped his scales with her heels and began riding him hard, cantering the way she had through fields her entire life.

Her body knew what to do. Instinct took over. Big Al moaned.

He wrapped his mouth around her injured shoulder, lapping at her blood as he thrust. Tanis became lightheaded with pleasure and blood loss. Big red tingling flowers bloomed through her entire body. She saw stars, again, whole galaxies in his iridescent feathers. She lost track of her orgasms, where one began and another ended; it became an endless chain. Could she die, she wanted to know, from too much pleasure? She hadn't believed it was possible. Then—when she thought it would never end, that they would stay like this forever—with one final explosive thrust, she felt his love go off like a rocket inside of her, filling her completely.

It was over. Big Al lay down in the field. She climbed up onto his chest and heard the deep pump of his heart, the braying of his breath. She knew she would love him for the rest of her life. He touched her temple again.

I'm so hungry, he communicated, and I-I-I- His thoughts stuttered, hesitant.

Go on, Tanis whispered, You can trust me.

I love the taste of your blood.

His eyes went shy as he said that. She felt his vulnerability. She lifted herself up to a seated position and looked down at her body, at the wound her father had inflicted on her shoulder. Her arm dangled, dead and grey. There wasn't any use trying to save it. She knew what to do. She offered her injured arm to his hunger and felt the hot pain of his love as he devoured the whole thing.

CHAPTER TWO

Tanis woke to the thin grey light of dawn. Cool wind brushed her ears and cheeks. After deflowering her in the hayfield, Big Al had picked her up and carried her all night pressed to his chest. When she asked where they were going, he had responded that he knew of a place just south of the Canadian border—a Dinosaur-human love sanctuary—where they could go and be safe. It sounded blissful to Tanis.

She felt dizzy and lightheaded. Her mouth was dry as sand. She looked down at her shoulder— Big Al's feather bandage was holding. All her life Tanis had grown up hearing the myth that dinosaur feathers had healing properties, but never had she imagined it to be true. The spot still ached, and she missed her left arm, but the bleeding had stopped and the wound didn't appear infected.

Big Al sprinted powerfully through the fields. Tanis felt small and in awe of him. When he ran, his lips curled back and the rising sun glinted a soft orange off his incisors. She had never respected or adored another being so much. The long grass shone in the early light. Silos cast long shadows. Tanis counted the cows they passed and started into their big trusting eyes—they were the only things she knew she would miss from her old farm life.

As they travelled, Big Al occasionally reached over and touched Tanis' cheek to tell her stories of his life. He grew up in a dinosaur nursery in Colorado. He and his three hundred and seven siblings roamed the Rocky Mountains, learning to hunt deer and fish in the rivers. He studied to be an electrical engineer and moved north because the tar sands offered him the best salary. He would've rather worked in dinosaur-human communications technology, but the money wasn't there.

For the first time ever, Tanis felt truly alive in her body. Everything excited her —the breeze, the smell of Al, the buttery sunshine. She felt renewed, baptized in sexual awareness. Big Al's deep panting from running made her thighs quiver. Halfway through morning, she couldn't stand it any more. She wiggled free of his arms and shimmied down his body. She dangled down with her ankles wrapped around his neck, her body along his. His sex hung like iridescent treasure, sparkling in the prairie sun. She stroked it. Al growled. Nervously, she licked it. Al stopped running, his sex inflating against her face. She licked more confidently. The dinosaur swayed on unsteady legs. She used her arm to stroke him while taking the tip of him in her mouth, running her tongue in wet circles around him.

He held her legs, so she was suspended upside down, and lowered his neck to lick her back. He breathed her in, smelled her deeply. His tongue entered her like an electric rod, sending sparks throughout her body. Her toes curled. They became one beast of licking and sucking.

Big Al stopped her, touched her to say, I want you completely. He let go of her legs. She slid down his body, landing face first onto the earth.

He bent her over and held her from behind with his talons. Tiny beads of blood rose to the surface everywhere he clawed her. The cuts burned deliciously. He entered her slowly, really making her feel the full mass of him. Again she felt like she would tear apart, her flesh melting off her bones, puddling in the field, but he gave her the time to open to him and her body eagerly accepted. She felt his heartbeat on her back. She was sure he would crush her, but she didn't. The only thing that crushed her was her own pleasure, undulating through her in waves.

Once finished, he picked her up again, held her to him, and they continued on. Could her life be like this always, running forever in the arms of her very own dinosaur?

It took them two days of running, interrupted only by Tanis' desire and the need for food and sleep, to arrive at the sanctuary. It wasn't what she expected. Instead of herds of dinosaurs and humans in various housing arrangements, she saw only one circular building in the middle of nowhere, a large log structure with many windows. An extensive vegetable garden bloomed and overflowed on one side of it. A few fields away, Big Al set Tanis down and they walked the rest of the way, side by side.

A few meters away from the sanctuary, Tanis caught sight of a figure running towards them, a female redhead in a simple brown dress. She was smiling brightly. Al left Tanis' side unexpectedly. He ran towards the girl and lifted her into his arms. Tanis stopped walking. Al swung the woman around several times before setting her on the ground. Tanis was about to start walking towards the couple again when, unexpectedly, Al tore off the woman's clothes, lifted her naked body and ran with her into nearby bushes.

Tanis couldn't breathe. What was she doing hundreds of miles from home, from all she knew? Her love—did she even know who he was?—had run off in the arms of a redhead. Tanis thought about the other woman. She was beautiful—tall and full-figured. Tanis' own chest seemed tiny by comparison. Through tears, Tanis saw another figure walking towards her, a woman with long black hair streaming down her shoulders. She was barefoot and wearing the same simple brown dress as the redhead.

"My darling, don't worry," she said when she was a few feet away. "It happens to all of us this way." The woman's voice was soft and breathy.

Tanis didn't know what to say. Who was this woman? She took Tanis' hand and led her towards the log building. Tanis was so disoriented from what she'd seen—what had she seen?—that she didn't completely register what was happening to her. She was only vaguely aware of the buzz of bees and earthy floral scent rising from the garden.

CHAPTER THREE

Tanis and the dark-haired woman entered the building through tall cedar doors.

Inside, the space was divided in two. One side was an oceanless beach of fine sand that drifted against the curved wall in a pillowy dune. The other was a field of soft grass with enormous cushions scattered across it. Light streamed in through the many windows, warm and gentle and glowing.

"This is our nest," said the woman.

Tanis blinked away her tears and took a deep breath. The air smelled like flowers, with that underlying fishy scent, and something else. Coconut? The woman smiled and stroked Tanis' arm. She led her to one of the cushions in the grass. "I'll show you," said the woman as she sat down, cross-legged, beckoning for Tanis to sit across from her. Tanis noticed that she was bare underneath her dress. Her pubic hair was like a dark tangle of roots. Her thick thighs were reddish-brown and dimpled over strong muscle.

Tanis sat down across from her. "You'll have to take those off," said the woman, gesturing to her clothes. "We don't allow Outside things here. We'll burn them later."

Still dumbstruck and mourning Big Al's betrayal, Tanis mutely complied. The woman watched as she set the torn ruins of her clothing aside, until all she was wearing was Big Al's feather bandage over the stump of her missing arm. The woman took Tanis' remaining hand and placed it between her legs, and placed her own hand between Tanis'. This was something Tanis had never done before, never even considered. But the woman's fingers began to move against her expertly and there was a gush of warmth and wetness and throbbing between her legs.

Tanis mirrored the woman's movements with her own hand. She found the nubbin of flesh that gave Tanis so much pleasure when Big Al licked it, and rubbed the woman's gently. The woman moaned and began to hum, then to sing in a language that Tanis had never heard. Her voice was light and liquid like sunlight in a stream. It echoed around the enormous chamber like a hymn.

This whole place is like a church, Tanis thought. But churches at home don't look like this.

Still singing, the woman opened her eyes and looked directly into Tanis'. Her irises were brown and flecked with bright gold. She got to her knees, pushed Tanis down onto her back, and nestled her face between Tanis' legs. She licked at the wetness there exactly as Big Al had, with a flat and muscled tongue, as if she was hungry.

Tanis' head spun. She felt herself responding, opening to the woman's insistent ministrations, but her pleasure was complicated by a stab of guilt as she thought about Big Al. His tongue had been so much bigger. How could he have left her? Was she betraying him too? "Big Al," she breathed through the pleasure of the licking and the pain of the betrayal.

"I know," said the woman, muffled, from between her legs. "Just wait until after the ritual." She entered Tanis with one finger, then another, then three. Tanis felt herself stretching deliciously with each added digit, as if she were a balloon, but she knew she could take more. And then, when her wetness flowed like a slow and salty river onto the cushion, the woman pushed her whole hand inside Tanis.

Tanis closed her eyes and cried out in pleasure and wonder. The woman's forearm was muscled and thick. Her fingers moved like tentacles inside Tanis, probing and rubbing the wet walls of her sex, an explorer in this soft pink territory. She was lightheaded with delight and with the smell of sex and fish and flowers. The woman resumed her licking at the top, swirling her tongue around as if Tanis were an ice cream cone. Between licks she made a series of high screeching sounds and low growls.

A minute later, Tanis heard the cedar doors open. She opened her eyes and stiffened, and the woman stopped her licking. Where was her modesty? Her sense of decorum? But that had all been left behind in Alberta, hadn't it? With the farm fields and cow dung and sunrises bright as a new penny. Her life was here now.

An allosaurus trundled through the door and made the same high-then-low call as the woman had. It was smaller than Big Al, with a white-and-yellow feathery halo. The allosaurus sniffed the air, crossed the grass and knelt beside Tanis to touch her temple.

Are you ready for the completion of the ritual? it asked her.

Tanis realized from its voice-feel in her brain that it was a female. She reached her remaining arm up to the allosaurus' face to stroke the dinosaur's shining skin. Sunlight refracted in the fluff of the iridescent feathers that grew everywhere, like prismatic wheat in an ancient field. The allosaurus gave a satisfied purr. Screw Big Al, thought Tanis. Two can play at this game.

Yes, said Tanis in her mind. I am ready.

The dark-haired woman slowly pulled her arm out of Tanis, wiggling her fingers and dragging against the sides of her all the way. Stars danced behind her eyelids as she gave a guttural cry, incoherent first with pleasure and then with the emptiness in its place. She writhed on the cushion's faded fabric, shuddering with the need to be filled. The woman moved to allow the allosaurus to settle between Tanis' legs, then straddled Tanis' upper body above her breasts. Tanis could feel her hot wetness against her chest. The woman's eyes were half-closed as she moved her body up further, positioning herself above Tanis' face. She smelled like sex, like spice and iron and honey and desire. Tanis opened her mouth hungrily, and at the moment her tongue met the woman's flesh, the allosaurus pushed her enormous dinosaur tongue inside Tanis.

They moved as one, humans and dinosaur, licking and stroking, tongues fluttering and rolling and tasting. Tanis had never been with a woman before, and she'd never really had the desire – but this woman tasted sharp and delicious, her juices flowing over Tanis' cheeks like excellent wine as she licked and sucked. Her ample thighs pressed against the sides of Tanis' face. And between Tanis' own legs, the dinosaur's tongue worked her into a frenzy. Her hips bucked as she pressed herself into the dinosaur's mouth, wordlessly pleading for more.

The woman sitting on Tanis' face stiffened suddenly as Tanis licked her in faster and faster circles, and gave a throaty cry as her orgasm gripped her. Tanis felt the woman's thighs clench rhythmically. It brought Tanis herself right to the edge; now she could concentrate on what was happening to her, on the dinosaur's tongue and its gentle rhythm, more insistent now as the pressure built.

Finally, after what seemed to be an eternity on the precipice, the saurian found the perfect spot inside Tanis, and beat her tongue against it in a fast rhythm. Tanis' orgasm exploded through her body, radiating out into every part of her. She screamed between the woman's legs; the vibration of her voice brought the other woman to another trembling orgasm.

Overwhelmed and sated, Tanis, the dinosaur and the woman collapsed into a heap, curled up together on the sand. Tanis drifted slowly and languidly off to sleep – but instead of the gentle peace and fulfilment she felt after sex with Big Al, there was a lack.

She wanted her dinosaur.

A single tear rolled down her cheek as she slipped into slumber.

CHAPTER FOUR

When she awoke, Tanis felt empty. She was hungry – when had been the last time she'd eaten? The vegetal scent of the garden drifted across her nose, all pease-blossom and earth. She was empty, too, of thick tongues and probing hands and other delicious bodily implements.

And her heart was empty. Big Al. His honky-tonk hair and his cocky stare, the smell and taste and size of him. His desire for her, the beating need of his subtly feathered body. The sheer Big Al-ness of him. He was a primordial jungle, verdant and hot and swelling, teeming with life. And he was a sex machine, pistoning into her like an oil derrick, to reach the thick and beautiful fluid that burst from within her in ecstasy.

Tanis groaned and turned over, and opened her eyes. She wasn't in the cathedral anymore; someone must have moved her. Instead, she lay on a soft mat on the ground in a tent-like structure not far from the garden, open at the sides and sheltered from rain by a white tarp "roof". In each corner, holding up the tarp, was a wooden pole carved into the shape of a detailed dinosaur phallus, complete with veins and ridges and carved drops of fluid that emerged from the tip.

She reached out and touched the wood, polished to a hard brown sheen and warmed by the sun. If she closed her eyes and stroked it just so, she could almost imagine that it belonged to Big Al. The throbbing between her legs started again. She'd never been so insatiable, she realized with sweet and terrible frustration. Big Al had changed her in some fundamental way. She hungered for the enormity of his sex, for the delicious pain and pleasure of his claws that raked her flesh. She touched the feather "bandage" on her injured shoulder and remembered his orgasmic delight as he'd crunched the bones of her arm, slurped the hot blood like wine, savored muscle and fat like it was a Wagyu steak at the kind of steakhouse where the servers make your individual Caesar salad at the table next to you. The tenderness he'd shown her as he repaired her torn and broken flesh and made her… not whole, but different. Smaller. Wiser. His.

And then she remembered the redhead, and her passion turned to grief.

There was a roar from inside the enormous temple, loud enough to rattle the windows in their brackets. The delicate leaves of the climbing pea plants in the garden, the soft little featherlike fronds of the carrot-tops, seemed to shake in terror. And then there was another roar, deeper and throatier, from another dinosaur, and a very human scream.

Tanis rushed to the doors of the temple, finding them open. Two huge male allosauruses faced each other across the enormous space, one on the grass and one in the sand. They stomped like sumo wrestlers from one clawed foot to the other, throwing clods of grass and clouds of fine sand into the air. Tanis was bitterly disappointed, but also relieved, to find that neither was Big Al.

A half-circle of women, including the dark-haired one who'd initiated Tanis, watched the spectacle. There was another scream from one of the women, a tall blonde with pale skin and spider-thin limbs – but Tanis realized that it wasn't a scream of fear or pain.

It was a mating cry.

The woman's voice ululated like a siren as she strode confidently between the dinosaurs. Her hair was the color of a buttercup in summer, her skin pudding-pallid. The brown dress moved with her body as she lay in the middle of the room, the upper half of her body on the sand, the lower half on the grass.

Together, the allosauruses lifted the woman, their swollen penises waving like little meaty flags. The allosaurus closest to her crotch plunged into her all at once, eliciting a squeal of delight from the buttery blonde, which was quickly muffled by the other allosaurus, who filled her mouth with his own twitching member. Together, they began to move, the woman filled entirely with dinosaur.

A cheer went up among the women. "I am Umber," said the dark-haired woman, "and I witness this joining. Who will second me?"

"I am Pine," said another, a stout woman with greying hair and a face so lushly beautiful that Tanis could barely stand to look at her, "and I witness this joining."

"We have two joinings today," said the dark-haired woman. "Bring in the others."

The cedar doors opened. A beautiful woman walked in: the redhead who had stolen Big Al when they had arrived. And behind her were two allosauruses.

One was Big Al.

Tanis' heart dropped. She felt nauseous. Her chest burned with a stuck cry of agony.

Big Al was as beautiful as Tanis remembered. His massive thighs were packed with muscle and his torso shone – had he been oiled? His cheekbones were carved from the finest jade. His cranial feathers were slicked back now in a vintage gangster style. The ridge of his neck swooped gracefully forward as he turned to look at her with those glittering sea-green eyes.

The redhead stood next to him, her chin high and haughty. She reached one freckled arm out to grasp Big Al's hand as if he were her saurian boyfriend. Tanis felt hot tears sting her eyes.

But Big Al shook the redhead off as if she were an annoying insect.

She squealed in dismay as she stumbled backwards. His haunches rippled as he leaped towards

Tanis, prompting an outcry from the gathered women. He ignored them. Gently, he touched her temple with his hardwired claw.

I didn't know, he said to her, grieving, pleading. I didn't know that humans so frequently pair-bonded.

Well, these ones don't, Tanis thought to him. But most of us do.

Are you angry at me? His thoughts were full of heavy woe. She thought she could see, just for a split second, a flash of an image from his mind, and could feel his experience with her: a point-of-view of her body bent over before him, little scratches beaded with shimmering and delicious blood, the incredible tightness of herself around him and the ramming, churning motion of their coupling. And then another flash: him with the redhead, her thin lips frowning, her stalk-like legs stiff and unyielding. The dryness of her, the crushing disappointment.

I can't love her, Big Al said. Is it because I only love you?

"Tanis," warned Umber. "This is a joining. It's not your turn. Keep away from the dinosaurs."

Tanis leapt into Big Al's arms like a piece

of popcorn violently released from its kernelled slumber and flung from a hot pan. He caught her lightly.

"My joining!" cried the redhead. "You get away from him!"

Big Al roared in her face, close enough to moisten her hair with the meaty sauna of his breath.

And then, together, Tanis and Big Al escaped through the cedar doors of the temple and began to run.

An evening prairie wind blew cold through the feathers that still clung to Tanis' ruined shoulder as they fled. Her sexual satiety from the woman and the allosaurus had long since faded, and the encounter had left her feeling empty and awful.

But the fact remained that she, like Big Al, had strayed from their love. She hadn't said no. She'd consented, whether from anger or bitterness or simply the hot slick friction of a tongue swirling in her most sensitive places.

"Big Al," she whispered to him as they cantered, several hours into their journey. "Will you forgive me? I didn't love them either."

Big Al stopped in the middle of a cornfield.

He crushed her tight against him, so hard that it blew the air from her lungs in a solid huuuuuuuh. Shall I show you how I forgive you? he asked, his mouth close to her neck. His scent was overpowering. His breath was salt and blood and heat, a glorious and primordial stink.

"Yes," whispered Tanis.

He lay her down between cornstalks that grew almost as tall as he was and pushed her brown dress up to her waist. Green-sheathed ears of corn bulged out from the stalks like hard uncircumcised penises. Yellow-brown cornsilk hung languidly from the end of each one, as if dripping. Big Al picked an ear and stroked the silk curiously, sniffing it. Then he tossed it away and knelt down with Tanis, grasping her hand with his wired one. He was already beginning to breathe harder. She felt as though there must be a puddle beneath her, so wet with wanting him was she. I will forgive you with pleasure, he said to her, and lifted her onto his swelling sex.

His sharp claws gripped her body. Her back and sides were alive with tiny burning points of pain that only heightened the pleasure that radiated from her stuffed center, like little salt crystals crowning a gorgeous silky caramel. Big Al's tongue licked her neck insistently, slurping up her sweat and the dirt that clung to her sticky skin. He folded her over forward like his own savory little tortilla and licked the drops of blood that ran down her back from where his claws had made divots in her flesh. She pressed her face against his lower belly, sliding against the soft iridescent feathers that grew like downy pubic fur on his skin. He made growly little saurian grunts from the depths of his throat and small birdlike peeps from his snout.

Big Al was moving inside her, stretching her to her limit, his sex rubbing over and over against the spongy ridged spot just inside her entrance. A new kind of pleasure built up, radiating along every nerve in her body as Big Al's cylinder of love pushed against the slippery walls of her deepest cave. His breath was raspy now, his tongue squashed against her back, dripping a puddle of meat-scented drool beneath them.

And then, almost simultaneously, their bodies shuddered uncontrollably with the power of their mutual climaxes, like tectonic plates during an earthquake. There was a spray of thin hot fluid from somewhere deep inside Tanis' body, mixing with the creamy film of her lubricating juices. She pulsed around Big Al's member, her muscles gripping and releasing, gripping and releasing, electric with pleasure like a slowed-down alternating-current outlet into which Big Al had poked his saurian shaft. She felt a firehouse-gush from Big Al's sex, squirting into her and stretching her even further with the sheer volume of his spunk. It spattered on the moist ground like a fall of heavy and gemlike raindrops, soaking the soil, puddling at the roots of the cornstalks that surrounded them.

Exhausted and exhilarated, the reunited lovers curled up together in the shadow of the corn as light drained from the cloudless sky. One by one, and then bunch by bunch, stars emerged into the rich and velvet darkness in their ancient constellations. Tanis pointed out the Big and Little Dippers, Orion with his phallic belt, Sirius the north star at his heel. A meteor streaked across the sky. Big Al gave a birdlike hoot of delight.

I never looked up at the sky like this back home, he told her as he pressed his claw gently to her temple.

Why? she asked.

Too much work. Always, always work. Never the time or space to look up. Or to think.

Can you think now? she questioned.

Sometimes. More and more. You make my mind clear. And my body happy.

Tanis snuggled against him. Even in summer, the night brought a chill to the field, and the clammy dirt clung to her skin when she moved. But Big Al's body was warm and nurturing. She nestled herself into the crook of his arm, threw one leg over his body and went to sleep.

CHAPTER FIVE

Tanis and Big Al awoke in the morning to the sound of rifle shots in the middle distance.

Tanis sat upright in shock, and then the fear hit her. A low growl started deep in Big Al's throat. Had her father and brothers somehow found her? Were they coming to finish what they'd started? She pictured her father's face, thin mouth twisted in a bitter scowl. His constant dismissal of her, his refusal to listen, to treat her like a human being. To him, she realized, she'd been no more than livestock, another mindless mouth to feed. But she wasn't mindless.

And neither was Big Al.

"We have to get away," she whispered to him, pulling the simple brown dress down over her burgeoning thighs. He nodded and sprang up with her in his arms, running away from the sound of gunshots, trying to keep his head down below the wispy tops of the cornstalks. But he was huge, and the green stalks rustled and snapped in his wake. Tanis grabbed a few cobs where she could, basketing them in the lap of her dress. They weren't great weapons, but perhaps they could provide a distraction. And they were heavy enough to hurt if they connected with a nose, she remembered from more than one Alberta night she'd spent cow-tipping with boys who'd gotten drunker than they should have.

There were shouts, though, and then the grind-cough sound of an engine revving. Big Al was fast, but he wasn't faster than a car at max speed. The sound grew closer. Big Al ran faster, his barbecue breath huffing.

They broke through the edge of the cornfield onto a rutted dirt path, dotted with large scum-filled puddles with gnats drifting lazily above in great clouds. A ragged-looking Jeep with tires too big for its frame barreled down the path towards them, not twenty feet away. Big Al leapt into action, but there was a sharp gunshot and a spray of blood from his right leg. He toppled with a keening cry, and Tanis went down with him, splashing into the warm and dirty water of the nearest puddle. The corncobs in her lap went flying.

Whoops and cheers came from the Jeep, which skidded to a muddy stop a few feet away. Three men in plaid shirts and jeans emerged from the vehicle. They weren't her father and brothers, Tanis saw with momentary relief, which was replaced immediately by terror and worry for her dinosaur lover, who lay sprawled and bleeding beside her.

"Got 'im," yelled one of the men in a broad Dakota drawl. He stalked towards the interspecies couple. His face was lined and leathery, though he didn't seem to be older than forty, and his eyes were flinty little specks.

"You been lookin' for one o' those!" said another of the men, a paunchy, droopy guy. His lower eyelids were bloodshot and pouched like a bulldog's. He gave a massive burp and pounded his chest. "Better out than in," he intoned.

"You want a job, buddy?" the first man snickered at Big Al. "Quarry ain't gonna dig itself."

"Look at his leg," said the third man, tall and broad and more soft-spoken than the other two. "You ain't done yourself no favors."

Big Al's lower leg bled steadily, but not profusely, from a set of two black-ringed wounds. The bullet had passed through muscle and skin and lodged itself in the dirt. He roared in pain and rage. The leather-faced man raised his shotgun. "Don't start thinkin' 'bout doin' anything stupid," he warned. He looked at Tanis. "This thing yours?"

She nodded mutely.

"He stupid?"

Tanis shook her head.

"Get in the car."

Tanis couldn't move. She was frozen with fear.

"I said, get in the car," the man warned, raising his shotgun again. Big Al gave her an encouraging chirp-growl. She put her head quickly to his wired claw as she stood up slowly. I'll be okay, he told her, in a combination of words and images. It's a minor wound. Go with them. I'll find you soon and we'll get out of here.

"What the fuck happened to her arm?" asked the droopy man with disgust. "Hey, lady, what the fuck happened to your arm?"

"A dinosaur and a one-armed chick," chuckled the leather-faced man. "It's our lucky day." He grabbed Tanis by her good arm, roughly but not violently, and marched her to the Jeep. He looked back over his shoulder and said to Big Al: "I'll be back for you soon, buddy. You're about to have a job."

The old bungalow farmhouse was about fifteen minutes over a dusty, bumpy road that snaked between fields. The men rejoiced at their good fortune over a background din of twangy country music and constant static. It seemed there was a gravel quarry at the edge of the property, and they'd been looking to hire a dino to do the heavy lifting. "But we got one for free!" the droopy man crowed nastily.

At the house, the leather-faced man shoved Tanis into a dingy bare-walled bedroom next to the kitchen and locked the door. There was a yellowed frosted-glass light fixture on the ceiling. Only one of the three bulbs was working, and that one flickered as if it were about to die. The bed was hard and springy, an old wooden bedframe with a mattress covered by a stained sheet and a colorful crocheted blanket. Cobwebs hung in every corner. An ashtray next to the bed overflowed with old cigarette butts; more cigarettes floated in a half-full glass of cloudy, tainted water. The room stunk of stale sweat and smoke and other, fouler body odors.

Tanis wanted to retch, but she knew she needed to keep her wits about her. She held her ear to the door and strained hard to hear what the men were saying in the kitchen.

"...happened to her arm?..."

"...pretty hot for a one-armed chick…"

"...can't fight back!..."

"...just a flesh wound, dinos heal quick, he'll be good to go by tomorrow…"

"...can't keep him in the barn, he'll eat the cattle…"

"...old barn on the hill, should be secure…"

"...chick is mine, I found her…"

A cold and horrible chill seized Tanis. She tried to imagine lying underneath the droopy-eyed man as he huffed and sweated above her, or looking into the flinty, narrowed eyes of the leathery-faced man as he held her one arm down. Even the tall man, who had seemed less malignant than the others, emanated a quiet danger.

She looked out the single grimy window. The

window-sill and casing were encrusted with dirt
and the sticky residue of old cigarette smoke, and
the rippled glass looked like it hadn't been cleaned
in decades. Nevertheless, she could see well
enough to spot what looked like a massive barn
atop a mound, its wood gray with age, surrounded
by tall grass and scrub bushes.

Carefully, Tanis braced her feet on the floor and
tried to pull the window up and open with her one
hand. Her heart thrilled for a moment as it moved
about an inch upwards, and then it stopped with a
loud crunching shriek.

Damnit!

There were footsteps in the hallway. Tanis'
heart hammered in abject terror. But it was the
tall, broad man who opened the door. He wasn't
handsome by any conventional measure – his eyes
were small and widely spaced, his nose piglike,
his chin narrow, his beard a patchy collection of
hairy wisps – but his expression was kind, if se-
rious. "Don't worry, boys, I got 'er," he shouted
down the hall. He pushed past a terrified Tanis and
closed the window. "Locked the damn window,"
he yelled – but he hadn't. He shook his head at
Tanis, and pointed at the drawer next to the bed.
Then he left the room, slamming the door and

locking it behind him.

"...get that dinosaur bastard," crowed the leather-faced man's voice, and then the men left the house. Tanis heard the sound of a much larger engine starting. A tractor? A pickup truck? She couldn't see from the window in here. But she kept her eyes on the decrepit barn on the hill to see if she'd been right. Sure enough, about a half hour later by her measure, a massive pickup truck dragged a horse trailer up the hill. She watched the men, small and insectlike from this distance, haul Big Al out from the trailer and prod him with their long rifles into the barn, before sliding the barn door shut.

With equal parts wild hope and sickening fear, Tanis opened the drawer that the man had pointed to. Inside was a packet of cheap cigarettes, a lighter, a few small packets of Kleenex, a beat-up low-end magazine full of naked women in improbable situations, and a large half-full bottle of something called PISTOL LUBE.

A full-body shudder overtook Tanis as she realized what the PISTOL LUBE was actually for, and what the fouler odor was: this room was full of stale, unwashed spunk. Had the man been giving her instructions so that she could make it easier for him to overcome her resistance? The thought made her dizzy with disgust.

But... her gut feeling told her no. He'd been kind. There had to be another reason.

The squeaky window!

Tanis took out a piece of Kleenex and gingerly opened the top of the bottle of PISTOL LUBE, then picked it up with her single hand. In the distance, at the top of the hill, the pickup truck was starting back towards the house; Tanis knew she had to be quick. She opened the window a crack, slowly, so as not to jam it. When she got to the stuck portion, she squirted a gob of lube with all her grip strength into the rail inside the frame on either side. She grasped the lift and pulled in a series of short bursts. The window opened a little wider, then came to a stop at about four inches open.

With a growl like Big Al's, Tanis squirted more lube. Thick drips cascaded down the crusted sides of the window-frame in a gross parody of arousal. Creakily, but steadily, the window opened even more, until it was open enough for Tanis to fit through.

The men were almost at the house. If she could

see them, they could see her, Tanis realized sickly. But they were laughing together, punching each other in the arms with hearty hillbilly humor – they were too preoccupied to notice the open window.

Now she just needed to get out before they put that horrible bed to disgusting use with her.

In desperation, Tanis looked around the room. It was almost empty: no closet, no furniture other than the bed and small bedside table. Nothing to bar the door. Nothing anywhere except that drawer.

Which held a lighter.

Tanis piled the crocheted blanket against the door to the room, ripped the magazine up into its individual pages – a few were stuck together, which made her shudder with horror – and placed the paper on top of the blanket as kindling. Girl Guides was good for something, she thought ruefully. She flicked the lighter and held it to one of the pages of the magazine, which smoldered and then caught alight.

The front door to the house opened just as the colorful fibres of the blanket began to burn. "Hey, girly," called the leather-faced man nastily. "Got a present for ya. It's hard as a rock, but it ain't a diamond." His footsteps came down the hall toward the room. "Hey, what's that smell? You a smoker? Hope you ain't smokin' my cigs, now, that's stealin'."

By the time he opened the door, Tanis was already out the window and running towards the pickup truck. The flames whooshed up into his face. "What the FUCK!" he screamed. "That was my mama's blanket! You bitch!"

Tanis had never run so fast in her life. She'd just barely missed qualifying for the provincial track championships back in high school, but she was pretty sure she'd have made it with her time in this particular race. The men, she noticed, hadn't even taken the keys out of the truck; they'd underestimated badly how desperate she was to get back to her dinosaur. She stepped on the brake pedal and gunned the engine.

Flames gouted from the window behind her. Burning bits of debris sailed off in every direction; one landed on the canvas roof of the Jeep they'd driven to fetch her and Big Al, and started it burning. The men shouted, running around outside of the house. Their screams grew fainter as Tanis drove the truck with all her might towards the barn.

The barn door was unlocked from the outside, but the latch was impossible to open from the inside. Big Al waited for her there, crouching in a corner in a pile of dusty straw and rotting wood. His leg had stopped bleeding, but he still limped as he cantered towards her. "Big Al," she cried. "We've gotta go!"

He touched his claw to her temple. Are they gone? he asked.

I burned the house, she said. And the Jeep. And I took their truck.

The dinosaur gave an amused chuckle-huff. You're more powerful than an eight-foot dinosaur, he said through their neural link, his "voice" soaked with pride. My fierce, beautiful little human girl.

Tanis leapt into the truck's cab. Big Al ducked into the horse trailer and closed it. And they drove towards the horizon, away from the farm, as the farmhouse burned behind them.

CHAPTER SIX

Tanis and Big Al traveled by night and slept by day for several weeks as the dinosaur's leg healed. She spray-painted the truck black, and Big Al helped her switch the license plates with a rusted old hulk of a 1960s VW Beetle she spotted in a ditch. A cigar-sized roll of twenty-dollar bills shoved by one of the men into the glove compartment of the truck represented her entire net worth. If anyone asked – and almost no one did – she claimed that she was an equestrian trainer who'd fallen on hard times with the loss of her arm, and was road-tripping back home to her parents' house in Kansas. "My horse doesn't like people very much," she said. "He's a kicker."

At Wal-Mart, she shoplifted new clothes, one

or two items per store to keep from being caught: gauzy slippy sundresses, a pair of shorts, a few T-shirts, a fuzzy fleece jacket for cold nights, a cross-body purse big enough to hold a few tampons and the truck keys. She'd never been a thief, not even in high school when the other girls were merrily stealing lipstick and eyeshadow from Shoppers Drug Mart and surreptitiously putting them on at school so their parents wouldn't object. But now she was an outlaw. She'd burned down a house to save her dinosaur lover. What were a few shirts from Wal-Mart in the grand scheme of things?

Tanis also became skilled at finding remote places to park during the day, because the horse trailer had become a love nest for her and Big Al. His heady fish-and-flowers scent permeated it, with the amount of time he spent inside. Tanis could barely enter without being overwhelmed by desire for him. And after a few days of healing, once his leg had lost its weakness, Big Al clearly felt the same way.

He grasped her in his claws and picked her up. She wriggled in delight. "I missed you," she said. "I missed this."

Big Al brought his face to her neck, to her

breasts, then sniffed between her legs. He rumbled a low sound of desire as Tanis realized what he wanted, and why.

"I'm on my period," she said. "You're hungry for the blood?"

Hungry, he said in her mind as he touched his claw to her temple. Hungry for you.

Tanis lay back against the wall of the trailer, cushioning herself with her fleece jacket, and parted her legs for her dinosaur lover. She smelled the metallic tang of the blood that flowed like a little iron-filled stream from her womb. Ethical consumption, she thought suddenly, and giggled.

Big Al gave a querulous grrrrrm?

"It's okay," Tanis told him, still laughing. "Just thinking about how perfect this arrangement is."

With a happy, sexy snuffle, Big Al buried his chiseled head between Tanis' legs and began to lick.

The pleasure was indescribable. Big Al was clearly hungry; he licked every drop of blood from between Tanis' thighs, and pushed his tongue into every crevice he could find, every fold, seeking out sustenance. His slick-but-rough tongue lingered at the top of her opening, where her clit lay exposed as he lapped at it insistently, long lick after long lick. He growled deep in his throat, and the vibration only heightened the sensation.

Tanis mewled in ecstasy, her hips writhing. Big Al reached out to steady her with his claws, drawing little pinpricks of blood, holding her in place for his searching tongue. Blood mingled with the juices of her arousal as he pushed his tongue into her, rolling and pulsing, pressing against every sensitive place inside her, trying to get more from her.

Her breath hitched as she lost herself in orgasm, clenching rhythmically around Big Al's tongue. But he didn't stop. The shimmering saurian growled again and pushed his tongue deeper, thickening it and rubbing it against Tanis. He pulled it out halfway and brought it back to her most sensitive bud, fluttering against it. The sensation nearly sent her into unconsciousness, her swollen flesh crying out for Big Al to stop, but also for him to keep going. "I… can't…" she whispered, so bound by sensation she was nearly speechless.

When she thought she couldn't possibly take even one more second of the overwhelming pleasure-pain, Big Al stopped. "No!" she cried, despite herself, and the dinosaur brought his tongue back to her, making tiny, almost impossibly fast flutters with his tongue. And then her body came undone. Warm juices squirted from a place inside her she hadn't realized existed. She was overcome by full-body shudders as hot electric pleasure coursed through her like a current. Her breath came in great gulps.

Her blood was smeared on Big Al's face like a joker's smile.

They lay tangled up in each other. Big Al had long since given up on slicking back the feathers on his head, and they stuck up in a sexy iridescent crest like an 80s club kid might have. "We need to get you a mesh shirt and bondage pants," Tanis murmured to him with a giggle as she stroked his warm and smoothly feathered chest, a jeweled meadow for her to explore.

They lay there languidly in the cocoon of the dark trailer, Big Al sniff-snorting contentedly. Tanis should have been enjoying the afterglow, but a persistent worry kept poking its way into her awareness: food. Big Al needed a lot of it and he wasn't getting enough. His skin had gained an odd slackness, his muscles had begun to tremble slightly with exertion, and even his gorgeous oil-slick of feathers had grown duller. The changes would have been nearly imperceptible to anyone else. But this was her dino-man. She'd grown to know every square inch of his body, from the thick keratinaceous claws to the powerful thighs that supported her weight as easily as if she were made of tissue paper, to the massive head and those green eyes whose depths she could only guess at.

Big Al was hungry all the time. He wasn't like her; he couldn't subsist on berries and on corn half-roasted on the truck's engine. He needed meat, and he wasn't getting it.

She realized that this was how much he loved her: he was desperately hungry, and still he didn't kill and eat her like the prey she was.

She needed to find him a consistent source of food, and fast.

Late that afternoon, at the next gas station, Tanis asked the bored-looking teen girl behind the counter where the nearest slaughterhouse was.

"Weird question," the girl said without looking up.

"Sorry," said Tanis, surveying the display of candy and gum. She could really use a Snickers, she realized, and decided to treat herself. She put the candy bar on the counter along with a twenty-dollar bill. "Just this, please. Yeah, I'm looking for a job. Usually the slaughterhouses are hiring."

This surprised the girl enough to peer over the counter at Tanis as she rang up the candy bar. Her eyes fixed on the mottled flesh of Tanis' shoulder, where Big Al's feather bandage had sloughed off to reveal a knot of scar tissue. "You sure? That's heavy work."

"I'm sure. I'm not squeamish and I can lift more than you think."

"All right," said the girl with a shrug, and pointed out the window to her left. "See that road? Take it about ten, fifteen minutes and then hang a right. Half an hour and you'll get to Old Morrison's. He's a character. He ain't gonna hire you for heavy lifting but maybe there's another thing you can do. Mop up blood and brains or something."

"You think he'd be willing to pay me in meat?"

"Lady," the girl said finally, "you ask a lotta weird questions."

Tanis ate the Snickers on the road, ripping open the package with her teeth. The sweet, rich taste of the chocolate was almost overwhelming. Perhaps this was how Big Al had felt as he gobbled her arm. Had it been like a candy bar to him? The decadent crunch of bone, the savory taste of her flesh?

Cornfield after cornfield sped by outside the window as Tanis drove. She hung a right at a signless intersection, as the girl had instructed, and kept driving. The setting sun hung large and low in a cloudless haze, pink and orange like the Slurpees that churned endlessly round and round at the 7-11.

She smelled the slaughterhouse before she saw it. The air slowly took on a miasmic thickness, redolent with the iron scent of blood and the fecal stench of dying animals. Back home in Alberta on her family's farm, Tanis' father and brothers had done the dirty work of the slaughterhouse runs with the steer. "It's unbefitting a lady," her father had told her. Tanis hadn't objected, preferring to spend time with the dairy cows, milking the life-giving liquid from their firm warm udders.

And yet here she was with her dinosaur lover, whose sharp-toothed maw was a graveyard, whose body ran on death. Death was what built those legs, those arms, that tongue that brought her so much screaming joy, his member that swelled so large and filled her so sweetly. Death was the engine on which her beloved was built.

And as the stark industrial buildings of the slaughterhouse drew closer, smokestacks belching foul ash, she knew would walk through the valley of its shadow, to give Big Al enough to eat.

CHAPTER SEVEN

"You only got one arm."

Tanis squinted at the man at the reception desk in the slaughterhouse's office building. He was shaped like a mound of meat scraps stuffed into his cheap collared shirt. His nose was covered with broken blood vessels and his breath smelled faintly of beer.

"I know," said Tanis.

"How'd you lose it?"

"Industrial accident."

The man guffawed. "Clumsy. How do I know you ain't gonna lose the other one in a machine here and sue us to kingdom come?"

Tanis stood up straight. "Sir," she said with more courage than she felt. "I work hard and I can lift a lot. You don't need two arms to push a mop. Besides," she continued, "aren't you an equal-opportunity employer?"

"You gotta Social Security number?"

Shit, thought Tanis with a mighty stab of fear. She hadn't thought about that implication of her Canadianness. "Never mind, sir. I'll be going now. Sorry for bothering you."

"Oh, it ain't a problem." The man's face had turned predatory. "Don't need papers to work at the slaughterhouse. Cash once a week, all the same to us. Just gotta keep me sweet on ya. Think you can do that, sugar tits?"

"Jimmy," came a booming voice from somewhere down a cavernous hall. "It ain't your place. Go out and have a smoke and come back when you got your cock under control."

The man hauled himself out of his chair and pushed through the glass doors into the gathering dusk. Another man, just this side of elderly, short and enormously stout with a round belly encased in a neon-print Hawaiian shirt, made his way down the hall towards Tanis. His moustache was glorious, a thick silver-grey bristle-brush across his upper lip. He had the confidence of a working dog in a herd of disgruntled sheep.

"Awful sorry, darlin'," said the man. "That ain't the way we do things here. You don't gotta look twice at Jimmy's ugly mug. You wanna push a mop, you can push a mop. Cash pay is weekly, every Friday. We got a deal?"

"I know this might sound a little weird," said Tanis. "But I… really like meat. A lot. Can you just pay me in meat?"

"Damn, I'm glad ol' Jimmy weren't here to hear you say that. He'd pay you in meat, all right." The short man rubbed his eyes.

"Maybe I can get all the offcuts? The cheap stuff. Intestines and kidneys and brains and all that."

There was a pregnant silence. The man rubbed his eyes again and stared intently at Tanis, as if looking closely enough at her would solve the mystery of the beautiful one-armed woman asking to be paid in cow parts. At last, he sighed. "Can't give you the kidneys," he said, "or the intestines, but you can have as many brains as you want. Can't legally sell 'em 'cos of mad cow disease.

You shouldn't really eat 'em either. But that ain't up to me. Tell you what: we'll pay you minimum wage and give you as many cow brains as you can fit in that little belly, and no one's gonna ask questions. Saves us from havin' to dispose of 'em."

"I can live with that," said Tanis.

"Alright, little lady. I'm Dallas Morrison," said the man.

"Tanis." She shook his hand with her good one.

"How do you feel about night shift? No better time'n the present."

"I feel," said Tanis, "like that suits me just fine."

What Tanis didn't expect was that Big Al would be discovered so soon.

"The fuck you got in there?" shouted Jimmy from behind her as she opened the door to the trailer to greet Big Al.

She'd parked the truck and trailer in the far corner of the lot near the Porta-Potties, in the hope that the same deliberate disinterest with which most humans regarded Porta-Potties would transfer to her vehicle. Unfortunately, it seemed that

Jimmy's interest in her was stronger than any sense of decorum.

"Did you follow me?" hissed Tanis.

There was a low growl from inside the trailer. Tanis hissed again, shushing Big Al, low and desperate. But it was too late. The dinosaur's enormous head was close enough to the doors that it caught the dim orange glow from a nearby parking-lot lamp-post, even as the last bit of daylight drained from the bottom of the sky. His feathered crest made a golden halo around the top of his head. His skin shone.

"Is that a dinosaur?" whispered Jimmy almost reverently.

"Yes," said Tanis, shortly. "He's mine. He belongs to me."

"He for sale?" Jimmy's eyes narrowed.

"Absolutely the hell not," growled Tanis. "He's bonded to me. He's mine."

Jimmy shrugged. "Suit yourself." He sauntered back inside the building.

Tanis breathed a sigh of relief. When Jimmy was out of sight, she jumped into the trailer and wrapped her legs and her good arm around Big Al, who nuzzled her in exactly the place she loved the most.

Tanis embraced him, bringing her eye in line with his. "I love you, Big Al," she murmured. She stroked his neck gently with her fingers, then ran them down his arms more firmly. His body-feathers brushed her skin softly like a thousand tiny kisses. She shivered with want.

She knew Big Al could smell her arousal, too. His breath was redolent of blood and bone marrow, a rich stench that Tanis had learned to love. She could feel his muscles tensing, could feel a swelling between his enormous legs –

There was a knock at the trailer door. "Hey, little lady," called Dallas. "I hear you got a friend in there who likes cow brains."

Both Tanis and Big Al immediately froze. It was bad enough being caught with a dinosaur – but being caught in flagrante delicto with a dinosaur would be much, much worse. "That's right," said Tanis loudly. "I'm just cleaning – cleaning him up. And myself. Getting ready for work." She combed her fingers through her hair, trying in vain to make herself look presentable.

I will protect you, said Big Al to her, touching her temple gently.

"It's OK," said Tanis in a low voice. "I got this."

"Pardon?" called Dallas.

"Oh, just talking to the dino," said Tanis, unlatching the trailer door and swinging it open to find Dallas standing there. "Have to keep him socialized."

Dallas looked intently at Tanis, and then at Big Al. "You're brave," he said finally. "And I got good news, dependin'. How well-trained is this guy?"

Big Al refrained from growling. He'd always been smart, Tanis thought, smarter than she'd ever imagined a dinosaur could be, but he was getting better at reading human interactions, understanding the intricacies of social dynamics. He was learning.

Of course, he'd always been good at reading her cues, when they were wrapped up together in an embrace. His tongue always knew exactly where to lick, how much pressure to apply. He always knew exactly the right way to touch her to make her scream in ecstasy…

She was grateful for the dark, suddenly. It hid her hardening nipples and her flushed cheeks.

"I don't know if you really train them," she told Dallas. "They're intelligent – they're more human than animal. But if you're asking whether... Big Dude... is a threat to humans, the answer is no. He's the gentlest dinosaur you could ever imagine. He'd never hurt anyone." Big Dude? Tanis felt a rush of embarrassment. What a stupid name.

"He didn't have nothin' to do with, say, a certain injury?" Dallas' eyes were sharp.

"Absolutely not," said Tanis firmly and truthfully. "That was a gunshot wound. All Big Dude did was help me bandage it up." And eat the remnants, she thought, but that was really none of his business. She'd have lost the arm anyway. And Big Al had enjoyed it.

If she was honest with herself, she'd enjoyed it too, in a faintly horrifying, never-to-be-repeated kind of way. There was something deathly sexy about watching Big Al consume a part of her like a tasty, meaty protein bar.

"So here's what I'm thinkin'," said Dallas. "That dino looks strong. Looks like he's suited to this kinda work. I want him to be my cow brain disposal. He's gonna crack the skulls and get the brains out so we don't gotta strip 'em out the hard way for bone meal. He'll get all the brains he can eat, plus a whole cow every week. And you, little lady," he said with a crooked grin and a wink, "you're wasted on broom-pushing. I think you're more of an office girl. How are you with numbers?"

By the end of the first week, Big Al's skin had plumped out again, and the sparkle was back in his eyes. Tanis was even getting used to the all-permeating stink of the slaughterhouse.

But what she hadn't had for a long time, and really, really needed, was a shower. Or a bath. Or something to get her clean. Big Al always claimed he was happy to lick her from top to bottom, of course, like a cat grooming another. But somehow Big Al always lingered on her nipples, which hardened to firm nubs under his ministrations, or on her ruined shoulder, whose scar tissue had become surprisingly sensitive to gentle touch. Or between her legs. Once Big Al had begun to clean her there with his lusty tongue, that was the end of the bath – and then, one or two or five intense orgasms later, she was sweaty and dusty again, and dripping with her own and Big Al's sex fluids.

So she and Big Al took a morning drive around to explore. Along a heavily potholed back road, they found an overgrown, abandoned-looking farm property with a dilapidated farmhouse and a scummy little pond fed by a weed-choked creek. When they followed the creek a hundred yards or so into the woods, though, they found its source: a clean, cold spring that gushed from a crevice between two large boulders, making a narrow but deep-looking pool at the stream's head.

Big Al touched her temple. It's like you, he said with a humor-filled snuffle. The rocks and the water. When you're wet.

"Big Al," Tanis giggled. "Did you just make a joke?"

It's true, though, isn't it? he said.

"Why don't we find out?" teased Tanis, dipping her good hand in the cold water and running it over his chest.

Big Al made a birdish whistle-wheeze. Cold! he said, emphatically. You're warmer.

"We do need to get clean," said Tanis. "At least, I do. Let's have a dip and then warm up together?"

Rather than answering, Big Al scooped her up

abruptly in his arms and plunged them both into the pool.

"Eeeeeeek!" The cold water was nearly painful on Tanis' skin, and her flimsy white Walmart dress clung to her, providing no protection whatsoever. Wherever her skin touched Big Al, though, was warm as a winter hearth. The contrast took her breath away – which was good, because Big Al dunked them both underwater, slicking her hair and his crest-feathers back as they rose again above the surface.

Tanis rubbed the water from her eyes, shivering from the cold and heat combined, and gazed at her dinosaur lover. Water beaded on his body-feathers, which seemed to serve the same function as a duck's, wicking the moisture away from his beautifully scaled saurian skin. Sunlight snuck between the treetops and illuminated the droplets like iridescent jewels, as if Big Al were a creature made entirely of sunshine and precious gems.

He belongs in a museum, thought Tanis. And then she realized the irony, and laughed to herself. He's here with me because he doesn't belong in a museum with all the fossils. He belongs to the world as it is now. He belongs to me, this creature of splendor, this meat-breathed, gleaming-eyed anachronism. How kind the universe is, to have delivered him to me in all his glory.

Big Al, noticing her reverie, brushed a strand of damp hair from Tanis' temple. What are you thinking about? he asked her.

"I'm thinking about how no one in the history of the world has ever been as lucky as I am," she whispered to him.

Big Al cradled her against him, hooked his hind claws against the side of the pool, and pulled them both out of the water. A broad sunbeam shone on a flat white granite rock, where he laid her on her back, and then sat back on his haunches, gazing at her. The sun was warm and strong, and within seconds, her skin had warmed and begun to dry. She knew that hunger in his eyes. It was nearly overpowering. She was dizzy from the sun and from her need for him.

"Come and get me," she said to him, low and throaty.

And then he was on her, wetting her with drops of water that showered down onto her from the feathers, a wild little fall of rain. Just as he'd done the first time they'd been together, he took his talons to her shoulders, pushing her roughly against him. His sex swelled and pressed at her opening, and then slipped in with little ceremony. It hurt the way it had at the beginning, a shock of pain and then a wave of pleasure as she split for him. His talons hooked into her shoulders with points of burning pain that glowed like campfires in her awareness, almost comfortingly. She belonged to him. She wanted only him. She needed him completely, in every possible way.

He rocked her on his sex, sliding her along its enormous length as she mewled for him in pleasure and delicious pain. He was tearing her, she knew, but not badly. And it would just give him more blood to lick from her soon enough. He was grinding into her as if she were the mortar and he the pestle. She gushed with the slick fluids of her own arousal, coloured ever so slightly with blood.

Big Al unhooked his talons one by one from her back, pulled her up so that she was pressed against his chest, and with his mighty tongue he licked the blood that flowed in small streams from the small tears in her flesh. Crazed now with bloodlust and sex, he pounded into her harder and faster, as if making her into mochi. Tanis had never felt so stuffed full, so complete, as if his enormous member was plugged into her, connecting her to the secrets of the universe.

And then the allosaurus gave a mighty carnivorous roar, a king of the world, as his orgasm overtook him. A hot jet of fluid spurted into Tanis like a firehose, nearly sending her flying, but Big Al held her to him; instead, the thick liquid splashed out of her, soaking her thighs. The force of it against her sensitive walls brought her close to her own orgasm, though she was still teetering on the precipice, shaking and moaning.

Big Al pulled out of her, brought his head between her legs and, gently and masterfully, whirled just the very tip of his tongue against her.

Tanis' entire body convulsed in the most powerful orgasm she had ever imagined possible. Behind her eyes were stars, galaxies, bright lights streaking across the sky. She screamed in agonized ecstasy, involuntarily, a pressure valve against the all-encompassing pleasure that would otherwise have swallowed her whole, deleting her entire personhood, leaving her to float forever in a sea of bliss.

Afterward, exhausted and barely conscious, drunk with delight, Tanis and Big Al curled up together in that same sunbeam.

There were worse ways to live, thought Tanis. She had enough to eat, a place to sleep, cash in hand for necessities, and a lover who thrilled her every day of her life.

She had everything she needed.

CHAPTER EIGHT

And then one late-summer evening, just as they were about to wake up for their respective night shifts, the interspecies lovers' peaceful sleep was shattered by the plaintive wail of sirens.

Blearily, Tanis sat up straight. Big Al, being a predator, slept lightly; he was alert and growling before Tanis had even registered what was happening. The horse trailer shook as he maneuvered himself protectively around her, with a clear bite-shot at whomever was dim enough to open the door.

The sirens grew louder and closer. Tanis' heart pounded. Maybe they weren't looking for her, she pleaded with the universe. She hadn't done anything wrong. She was an adult. Big Al was an adult. They had every right to live as they chose.

But as Tanis knew from growing up in rural Alberta, what was allowed in theory and what happened in practice were often two very different things.

The wee-oo of the sirens grew almost unbearably loud, amplified by the sheet metal of the trailer, and Tanis heard the sound of tires on gravel as the cars pulled up to their spot near the Porta-Potties. Big Al was growling like a guard dog on duty, snuffling rich cow-brain breath through his nostrils. His thick and muscled thighs were taut and ready to spring. The soft feathers that covered his skin stood on end, like a tiny army of iridescent soldiers at attention. Golden-hour light poured through the barred-slit window at the top of the trailer. He looks like a dinosaur god, thought Tanis, like an avatar of the divine on earth. He was so beautiful she wanted to cry.

I can't lose him.

There was talking, now, and the slamming of car doors. "Tanis," shouted a deeply familiar voice. "Tanis, are you in there?"

Shocked to her core, Tanis froze. No way. No way was this happening.

"Tanis?" came the voice again.

Big Al growled louder, almost a snarl-roar.

"No one's going to hurt you," said the voice. "Tanis."

"......Dad?" Tanis half-whispered, querulously.

"She's in there," her father said to someone. "And she's got that goddamn dinosaur with her."

Tanis felt sick. She clung to Big Al. "If you go, I go," she whispered to him. "I don't want to live without you."

Big Al touched her temple. Don't say that. His inner voice was calm, but there was a runnel of fear barely hidden just below the surface.

"Dinosauromeo and Juliet," whispered Tanis with a hysterical giggle.

I read that play during language training, said Big Al in her mind. It wasn't a love story. It was a tragedy about two teenagers making stupid decisions. We don't want to emulate it.

As Tanis' mind was boggling with the thought of her dinosaur lover having read Shakespeare, there was an enormous metallic crash, and the doors to the horse trailer bowed open.

Four police officers stood with their guns drawn in a half-circle around the back of the trailer. Tanis' father stood in the middle, arms crossed, scowling. And next to him stood Jimmy, a nasty little half-grin playing at the corner of his mouth.

"That's the girl," said Jimmy to the officers, pointing at her. "She's right there. Looks just like the photo I saw on the Internet."

"That's her," cried Tanis' father. "He's right. That's her. Tanis, it's time to come home now. Get that shoulder looked at. See your brothers. We've missed you."

Of course, in the missing-person poster he'd spent the past few months putting all over every physical and digital space he could find, Tanis' father had neglected to mention how she'd lost her arm.

"And that's the dinosaur, too," said Jimmy. "He's a nasty fucker. Probably best to put him down, no need to risk anyone's safety."

"No!" screamed Tanis. "He's no danger to anyone! Big Al is gentle! He's loving. He's wonderful."

"That may be so," said one of the officers, "but standard protocol with a carnivore is that when there's an issue like this, we take them into our custody to keep everyone safe. Come with me, please, sir," said the officer to Big Al as Jimmy grinned triumphantly. He winked at Tanis.

Big Al growled low in his throat.

"Now, sir, let's not have that," warned the officer, raising a Taser.

Behind him, a few hundred feet away, a short figure emerged from the doors of the office and began to half-run, half-waddle towards the commotion.

"Please come peacefully," said the officer to Big Al.

"He tore up my daughter," growled Tanis' father. "Ran away from the farm with her. Stole her. And it looks to me like he ripped her arm clean off."

"That was you," sobbed Tanis, "with your gun. You shot me. Big Al saved my life. All he's ever done is love me. He loves me more than you ever have."

"Is this true?" asked the police officer with the Taser, looking at Tanis' father and lowering the weapon slightly.

"I…" Tanis' father began. The figure running towards them from the office building grew closer.

"That's a lie," interrupted Jimmy. "This bitch is a liar. She's stealing from the company. I saw it myself. Did the books. Embezzlement. I was gonna fire her today, and that slimy lizard boyfriend of hers, too. No-good thieves. Send 'em back where they came from. We don't need this kind stealing jobs from good hardworking Americans. I swear to…"

There was an enormous thwack as Dallas Morrison, breathing hard from the exertion of running to the edge of the parking lot from the main building, wearing an eye-wateringly neon yellow Hawaiian shirt and khaki cargo shorts, cracked Jimmy across the back of the head with a thick metal binder full of paperwork.

The sneering man stumbled, stunned, and slumped to his knees against the nearest Porta-potty.

"What," boomed Dallas, "in the god damned fucking hell is the meaning of this?"

Big Al roared and growled. The police officers wheeled towards Dallas, guns out, but when they saw who it was, they lowered their weapons.

"Dallas, they're trying to kidnap Big Al," Tanis cried. "And my father is trying to kidnap me! But I don't want to go! I'm an adult! I won't go!"

The police officers stared at Dallas with wide eyes, the whites showing all around.

"Mr. Morrison," said the tallest one, a brown-haired, nondescript man of about thirty. "Are these… folks… your employees?"

"They are."

"Jimmy claims they were stealing."

"That's a lie, sure as I'm a Morrison like my father and my father's father before me. And I surely don't appreciate y'all comin' on down here and lettin' some guy," he gestured to Tanis' father, "lay hands on a lady, employee or no. Y'oughta be ashamed of yourself."

"I'm her father," growled Tanis' father.

"And I'm her boss," said Dallas, "and she's a grown woman, and last I checked, the laws of these good United States of America indicate that once a person reaches the age of majority, that is, eighteen, they are free to make their own decisions without the input of their parents. How old are you, Tanis?"

"Eighteen," said Tanis. "Almost nineteen."

"You see?" said Dallas, turning to the tall officer. "She's eighteen, almost nineteen. And she does not want to go with her daddy."

"She's been missing for months!" shouted Tanis' father aggressively. "She's just a girl! She's naive. And she's Canadian! She can't have a job in the United States! Can't you extradite her?" he asked the police officer, desperately. "She needs to come home and learn her lesson."

"Is this true?" asked the officer to Dallas.

"I don't see anyone missin'," said Dallas. "Last I checked, the girl's right here in front of y'all."

"But she's Canadian."

"I'm sponsoring her visa," Dallas said with finality. "And the dinosaur's. You don't like it, you take it up with Homeland Security. But I think you'll find the papers are all in order."

The officers looked at each other.

"Sir," one finally said to Tanis' father, "let's get you back home. It seems as though your daughter wants to stay where she is."

"What the fuck?" screamed Tanis' father.

"What the fuck do you mean? She's gonna stay here with that thing? Do you know what she's doing? With that creature? She's a sick puppy. Girl," he shouted at Tanis, "you are one goddamn sick puppy. You're no daughter of mine. I don't want you. You stay here now, you don't ever come home, you hear?"

"Sounds like a plan," said Tanis.

The officers turned away and bundled Tanis' father into one of the cruisers. Lights on but sirens off, they drove off down the road the way they'd come, a whirling blur of blue and red shrinking against the darkening horizon.

"And now, Jimmy," Dallas said to the half-conscious man slumped against the Porta-potty, "once and for all, let's deal with you."

Jimmy glared at Dallas balefully.

"Here's the thing," said Dallas conversationally. "There's a lot about you I don't like, Jimmy. I've put up with a lot from you because of who your mama was and who your daddy wasn't. More 'n anyone else has ever tolerated. But I ain't puttin' up with it no more. You just lost your last friend."

Jimmy spat blood, glaring at Dallas defiantly.

He looked over at Tanis and licked his lips suggestively. "She should be mine," he lisped through blood-speckled saliva and broken teeth. "This is your fault."

"Jimmy," said Dallas. "Jimmy, my boy. I don't like a lech. I don't like a snitch. But most of all, I don't like a man who tries to destroy a woman because she don't want 'im."

The police lights faded further into the distance.

"One day," sneered Jimmy. "One day your ass is mine, lizard. And you, girlie," he spat at Tanis, with narrowed eyes, "you're gonna wish you'd said yes. I ain't gonna hold back. How're you gonna fight me off with one arm, once your lizard boyfriend is dead meat?"

That was it.

With a mighty Jurassic roar, Big Al pulled Jimmy in two like a piece of moist pink saltwater taffy. He popped the still-screaming head from Jimmy's torso as if opening a soda-can tab, and with a snort of disgust, tossed it down the foul hatch of the Porta-potty.

The next day– after burying the rest of the late unlamented Jimmy in a shallow grave behind the

Porta-potty— Tanis and Big Al got the keys to their own place.

"Ain't no one even inquired 'bout this property in the dozen years since I put it up for sale," said Dallas Morrison as they pulled up to the dilapidated farmhouse on the acreage where Tanis and Big Al had found the sweetwater spring in the woods. The FOR SALE sign still hung crookedly on a remnant of wooden fence at the front of the property. Tanis and Dallas got out of the truck and opened the horse trailer to let Big Al out. "Not enough clear land for farmin', and it'd be expensive to take that forest down. I think the real estate agent died a couple years ago, truth be told. But it's no skin off my nose. The place ain't doin' much but sittin'."

"I still can't believe you'd just give it to us," said Tanis, taking Big Al's claw in her hand as his other forelimb gently stroked her hair. "And honestly, I can't believe you're as unbothered by — by us — as you seem to be. Everyone else seems to call the cops on us. Or shoot at us. Like my dad."

"You know what?" said Dallas, looking from Tanis to Big Al and back again. "Seems to me that dinosaurs are intelligent creatures. Basically people, I reckon. And I ain't gonna object to how people love each other. We settled that piece a long time ago. You just tell me if any soul bothers you and I'll make sure they ain't gonna be able to do it twice."

Tears burned in Tanis' eyes all of a sudden, and a tangled, complicated bezoar of emotion rose in her chest. It was as if everything that had happened since she'd met Big Al — hell, everything that had happened since she'd started drawing dinosaurs as a teenager and those feelings for them had awakened in her, that awareness of their beauty and power and allure — was hitting her all at once. She was overwhelmed by the love she felt for Big Al, by gratitude to Dallas, by relief and guilt and sorrow about her father, all mixed together in a great stew of grief.

She knew she would spend years working through all of it.

But now, at least, she knew that she and Big Al would have the years to spend... together.

Maybe life on the farm could be wonderful, after all, on the right farm. With the right dinosaur.

And there was something else she wanted to talk to Dallas about: something she'd been looking into during her long nights in the office, that she and Big Al had discussed in every detail they could think of — that, if they could make it work, would change all their lives for the better.

"I have a proposal for you," she said to Dallas.

"A proposal?" The stout man's eyes crinkled in a smile. "I sure am curious 'bout that."

"For a new kind of slaughterhouse. With dinosaur workers instead of humans. It would be so much better for everyone, and more efficient, and healthier..."

"You know, Tanis," said Dallas, "I knew I hired you for a reason. Let's have a chat. But first," he said, gesturing to the little house, "let's get y'all home."

EPILOGUE

"**I** know," said Tanis. "I don't think you should need to wear clothes either. Trust me, I prefer you without them. But human business customs can be rigid."

Big Al grunted.

"These are venture capitalists," said Tanis. "They want to know one thing: will they make money on this deal? Your job is to make sure they understand that the answer is yes."

Big Al gave a meaty-fragrant whuff.

"We're gonna close this deal," said Tanis. "I know we will. As long as you wear clothes."

Big Al rolled his eyes – where had he learned to do that? – but complied.

Tanis sidled up next to him and looked at them both in the full-length mirror on the back of the hotel closet door. "You look good in a suit," she breathed. He did. His powerful tail emerged from the back of a dinosaur-sized-and-shaped pair of finely woven suit pants, and a matching suit jacket was cut perfectly for his arms and barrel chest. Shimmery threads in the linen of his shirt set off the iridescence of his feathers, and he'd styled his fine feather crest in the Elvis curl she'd fallen in love with…

How long ago now? It had only been three years, but it felt like a lifetime.

And you look good in that dress, Big Al said, touching her temple as he brushed a strand of honey-colored hair away from her face.

"Tan…is," he said out loud, slowly, in a halting rumble from deep in his chest. "Tan…is."

Tears sprang to Tanis' eyes, so overwhelmed was she with a sudden wild joy. "You can speak?" she breathed, shakily.

"Tan…is," said Big Al, more strongly this time. And into her mind, with a gentle touch: I'll never be able to speak like you do. But I want to learn as much as I can. And I wanted my first word to be your name. I love you, Tanis.

Tanis embraced him, every cell in her body crying out with delight. "I love you, Big Al," she whispered. "Now let's do this thing."

"There is a specific type of PTSD," Tanis said to the group of seated VCs, "called Perpetration-Induced Traumatic Stress, or PITS." She clicked to the next slide. "We're used to talking about PTSD in the context of people who are the victims in a traumatic situation, or are involved in trying to help. For instance, people involved in a car accident, or victims of crime – I've got some personal experience with that," she gestured to her armless left shoulder with her right hand, "or first responders. What we don't often think about is the traumatic stress experienced by people who engage in killing for a living: in particular, workers at the slaughterhouses that provide billions of people with the meat they want on their plates every day."

Tanis tried hard not to let her nervousness show. She knew that she and Big Al were on the right track. She knew that their idea would revolutionize agriculture. And she also knew that these people, looking at her impassively, were at least twice her age and had a whole lot more experience in business than an Albertan farm girl who fell in love with a dinosaur.

Her gaze rested for a moment on Big Al, who sat on his haunches at the back of the airy, many-windowed room. He waved one claw at her and pushed his head forward encouragingly.

"One of the most common causes of PITS in humans," said Tanis, "is working in a slaughterhouse. Killing animals day in and day out. And the research shows," she clicked to the next slide, "that slaughterhouse workers are far more likely than the general population to experience anxiety and depression, develop substance use disorders, and perpetrate domestic violence and other forms of violent crime. It does something terrible to us."

A few murmurs from the room.

"That's why," Tanis said, "we're proposing a plan, in partnership with Morrison Meats, to replace all human slaughterhouse workers with dinosaurs, and to replace the current slaughterhouse model with one that's much more humane for the animals and is designed for dinosaur workers."

"We already have a successful pilot program in place at our primary abattoir near Springfield, South Dakota, and we're planning to roll it out to two more Morrison facilities in the next three months. We've secured sufficient dinosaur employees for six more," said Dallas' voice via a speakerphone on the table, crackling slightly. "We only expect the demand to grow."

Tanis clicked to the next slide, a photo of allosauruses at work on the slaughter line, along with a few very telling graphs.

There was an explosion of chatter from the dozen or so VCs. "I know what you're thinking," said Tanis as they quieted down. "How will we keep them from just eating all the animals? What about trauma to the dinosaurs? Won't killing all day stoke their bloodlust, make them more dangerous?"

"Those are certainly questions that need answering," said a dark-skinned woman in a white skirt suit, sitting at the front, "but I'm intrigued."

"Here are the answers, one by one," said Tanis, clicking to a slide with graphs. "One, dinosaurs are hungry creatures, yes, but they aren't bottomless pits. The small amount of animal loss is far outweighed by the savings represented by having a healthy, happy workforce best suited to the job. Which brings me to two: carnivorous dinosaurs are natural-born predators. Killing isn't traumatic to them the way it is to social omnivores like humans." She took a deep breath and clicked to the final slide.

"As for that last question: dinosaurs who've been properly socialized with humans are no danger to us. Dinosaurs are intelligent creatures, as smart as us. They're our friends. They're our family. They can even be... beloved."

She gazed at Big Al, who looked back at her with his deep green eyes and what she could swear was an almost-human smile.

"Invest in our dinosaur-powered slaughterhouse model," said Tanis, "and the world will be so much better for everyone: animal, human and dinosaur alike."

The next day, back home on their fixer-upper farm, as she paced back and forth in front of the window and waited for a phone call, Tanis saw a crack beginning to form in a particular enormous egg.

The egg had come to them from a working-dino housing facility in Pennsylvania, where a mining accident had killed three allosauruses, including both parents of this particular chick-to-be. The mother had been a clutchmate of Big Al's. Other dinosaurs at the mine had adopted the other eggs, as was the standard procedure, but the last one had come to Big Al via a whisper network of dinosaurs that Tanis barely understood.

She wasn't quite sure what to make of it, but Big Al was entirely confident in his parenting skills — and hers. You'll figure it out as you go along, and I'll help, he told her, brushing her hair away from her temple. Like parents have done since the beginning of time.

"As someone whose species is much closer to the beginning of time," said Tanis with a slight smile, "I trust you." Big Al had growled at this, but with humor — and the two had ended up in precisely the kind of situation that would have created a child in other circumstances.

And now, there was a crack. It was tiny, hairline and nearly invisible in the mottled roughness of the shell, but it was unmistakable. Tanis opened the oven-sized incubator, the egg as high as her waist, and traced it with her finger to be sure. Yes, it was a crack, all right.

"Big Al!" she cried. "Big Al! It's happening! The orphan egg!"

With a pounding of footsteps, Big Al thundered

across the house and nearly skidded as he reached the incubator. He poked a claw gently, so gently, against the egg, and then tapped it.

The egg gave an almost imperceptible shake, as if its occupant was tapping back.

Big Al made a noise Tanis had never heard before, a high, birdlike cheep. He tapped the egg again; again, it shook. A spiderweb of cracks blossomed.

Tanis' cellphone made a bloop. She tore her eyes away from the egg and glanced at the screen. The email preview was enough.

"Big Al. It's a yes. They're going to fund it!" she cried. "Thirty-five million! I have to call Dallas!"

His reply was drowned out by an enormous krrrrrrrrack as the egg's thick shell split wide open. As Tanis and Big Al stared open-mouthed, a small wet head emerged, slick with the sticky fluid inside.

The allosaurus chick gave a puppylike shake of its head, splashing little droplets across the lovers' rapt faces. Then it looked from Tanis to Big Al and back again, and made that same birdlike cheep.

I see you.

"Little Al," crooned Tanis.

"Li…ttle," rumbled Big Al.

The new family stood by the window, bathed in the golden light of late afternoon as they welcomed new life into the world – just as their ancestors had done for millions, billions of years, basking in joy and bliss under the warm and loving gaze of the very same sun.

Lord Bartholomew's Ankylosaur Lover

IN THIS VOLUME

IN FORTHCOMING VOLUMES

CHAPTER ONE

Lord Bartholomew woke up tangled in his ruby silk sheets, sweaty and forlorn. Last night's date had been a bust, as always. He had admired Lady Agatha's tall stature, broad shoulders, no-non-sense long, straight nose and narrowed eyes from across the room at balls for months.

The cousin of a German Count with English land, she had been imported from the Rhineland to be displayed for potential suitors with adequate land, title, and wealth.

Two weeks ago, Lord Bart tip-toed across the white marbled floors of Lord Wilhelm's mansion, carrying two brimming glasses of champagne. He passed one to Lady Agatha, who looked down at the shorter, more narrow Lord Bart without a word, lips pursed, her countenance as full with skepticism as the glassware was with champagne. However, he regaled her with tales of his family's deep roots in English aristocracy and invited her to summer at each of their eight castles – dotting the English countryside like wayward sheep.

"*Ja*," she purred, "*Acht*, very impressive."

She even agreed to meet him for dinner at a glamourous schnitzelhaus reserved for the upper crust, complete with bite-sized wieners served on two-pronged golden forks and beer imported from the depths of Cologne.

Lord Bart hustled to the date (in his family's carriage, of course,) with tight pants, a meticulously personalized love poem tucked under one arm, and the intent to woo.

When he arrived, Lady Agatha was already seated, swirling a glass of sweet Gewurztraminer with one elbow propped on the table. He imagined his head crushed between her striking thighs, herself as sweet as the wine.

The chit-chat over dinner seemed to go well, though she didn't stray far from topics of his land ownership and his father's import-export company, how many ships were in his fleet and their monopoly on the finest grade silk imported from the Asiatic continent. He tried to sway her to topics such as Lord Byron's latest book of smashing poetry or the botany club's expansion into appropriating turtles from the moors and walking them on leather leashes through the bustling streets of London.

After a quick dessert of traditional German cake with seven layers of cream, topped with an embalmed cherry, Lord Bart offered her a tour of London in his carriage, (which he hoped to end with the great lady supine in his imported silk sheets, redder than the rouge on her broad cheeks.)

He fisted his poem, crushing the sheet of parchment he scribed it upon. He would read it to her; she would swoon.

He heaped her fur coat onto her shoulders and waited while she tucked her arms into the sleeves. Then, he opened the door for her and followed her onto the wet, cobbled street.

Night stroked London with the blurred, bleary reflections of streetlamps and moonlight filtered through a haze of woodsmoke and fog. Lady Agatha strode to the curb ahead of Lord Bart, and instructed the concierge to summon her carriage.

"Lady Agatha," he hurried to stand at her elbow,

"I wrote a poem to celebrate our first evening."

He smoothed the parchment clutched in his fist and cleared his throat:

"Lady Agatha, my German cake

Your body is rich as cocoa

Hot - fresh from the kettle, boiled

Over the fire of my loins

Join me at the warm hearth

In my bedroom

Let the heat bake us both

Between the sheets."

Lady Agatha's upper lip curled. She declined with a wave of her hand.

"But, why?" he said, his fingers uncurling and the poem falling to wilt in the dirt snow heaped at the curb.

"You're a dandy, Bartholomew," she said, "a Coxscomb. Ladies do not take such men seriously -

with your fancy dress and poetry."

She sneered. He still wanted to lean up and kiss her. Shame and the heat of inadequacy coloured his guts. They waited for their separate carriages on the street.

* * *

Lord Bart rang the copper bell he kept on his bedside table. Aragon, his French butler, padded down the hall and opened the door, smooth, without a creak.

Aragon was tall, blonde, with a roguish beard Lord Bart regularly threatened to make him shave – purely out of spite. He had a long, strong nose and a small mouth that offset his aggressive cheekbones. His figure cut a similar structure: broad, strong shoulders down to a set of narrow hips that still held suggestion. Every scullery maid in the damn household blushed when Aragon glided past.

"My lord?" he said.

"What? What do you want?" Lord Bart's original desires faded beneath his seething jealousy.

"You rang, my lord," said Aragon, calm.

Lord Bart fought with his sheets. He kicked them off and his silk pajama pants caught and dragged with the sheets, leaving him in bloomers. He stood on his bed, took a stance of authority over the butler.

"Right, Aragon," he said, "hungover, you understand. Very hot date last night."

"Of course, my lord," said Aragon, "shall I send Molly up to sponge bathe the sweat away from last night's exertions? Did you slip in through the window before morning's first light, young rascal?"

Lord Bart considered stretching the tale, regaling waifish Molly with riveting details of an imaginary tryst - sweaty and powerful - as she rubbed a sponge over her young master. He considered punching his inner thighs when Aragon left the room to raise convincing love marks to impress her. Molly was a sweet young thing, but not his type - too fragile looking, like a candlestick. Nothing enticing about a candlestick.

Lord Bart shook his head.

"No, my lord?" said Aragon.

Yes, Aragon. Lord Bart had forgotten the conversation. He signed; there was no longevity in lying to his trusted confident and well-paid best friend.

"Aragon, I'm a lonely, dirty liar." Lord Bart threw himself down on the sheets, burying his face in the stack of pillows. "She spurned me. She... she called me a Coxscomb!"

Lord Bart sobbed. Why didn't tall, handsome women respect him? Strong women with muscular bodies set his blood boiling, but they all regarded him as paltry, pale, weak - the way Lord Bart viewed waifish Molly. Life was unfair.

My lord," Aragon moved to the edge of the bed and set a hand on Lord Bart's quaking shoulders, "have you considered pursuing maybe a smaller woman? Someone of more feminine incline who might appreciate your cravats and poetry?"

Lord Bart shook his head. It was hopeless.

Aragon selected an outfit for him. He guided his heartbroken master down the oak spiral staircase to the dining hall. Molly brought him a tray of boiled quail eggs, thick slices of bacon, fresh baked bread, champagne, and an entire trout. He picked up his folded napkin. The fabric gritted between his soft fingers. He flung it to the cobbled floor.

"Molly! The quality of this linen napkin is arbitrary!"

Molly picked up the napkin, barely suppressing a disrespectful sigh, and faded back to the kitchen for a replacement.

"Apologies, my lord."

Lord Bart propped his elbow on the table and his chin upon his fist. What would he do today?

What would take his mind off the daggers pricking his heart?

"Aragon," he bellowed, "I'm sad! What trifles does London offer to distract me on this dark day?"

Aragon appeared in the kitchen doorway, where Molly had disappeared. Flirting, no doubt.

Everyone had a bedmate but him. The world was a cruel and unfair curse upon him.

"Did my lord not read the mail I sorted for him last week? You're an esteemed guest for the grand unveiling of the new exhibit at the zoo this evening," said Aragon.

"The zoo? How boorish."

Lord Bart pushed his plate of quail eggs and trout away, drawing closer his morning champagne.

"Perhaps not," said Aragon, "the new animal is very exotic - a new species discovered on one of Sir Russell MacDonald's dangerous forays at the Amazon. It is said the beast is so heavy the ship dipped down in the ocean until the deck nearly kissed the waves."

Lord Bart sipped his champagne. "What kind of animal?"

"No one knows," Aragon said, wiggling his fingers in a ghastly manner.

"Very well," said Lord Bart, "it's something to distract, I suppose. What's the dress code?"

Aragon shrugged. "Semi-formal, I assume. You'll be the best dressed, as usual."

CHAPTER TWO

The carriage rumbled along Finchley Road to the London Zoo. Lord Bart swayed with the ricochets of the wheels bumping along the uneven cobbles.

He wore a knee-length red velvet coat with shiny brass buttons, billowing silk trousers, and a fine linen shirt that clasped his throat with ruffles. Frills dripped from his wrists. He swept the curtain away from the carriage window and watched the late afternoon scatter past, lighting a thin cigarette of clove and tobacco, blowing smoke into the lonely darkness inside the carriage, where he sat alone.

Always alone.

He imagined the perfect female: powerful, with broad shoulders and a muscled stomach. Thick, strong thighs. Thighs that could crush his head like a watermelon. The allure of a voice purring a low vibrato. A female that could render him helpless and hold him in complete domination.

Lord Bart was just about to unlace his trousers and slide his hand down to relieve himself – he was, after all, alone, and it was *his* carriage – when the carriage jerked to a halt. He dropped his cigarette on the plush floor of the coach and hurriedly stomped it out.

"The zoo, milord," called Frederick, his coachman. The carriage door swung outward and a small brass ladder unfolded to the ground.

Lord Bart exited. The tall iron gates of the zoo stretched twelve feet high and ended in fat barbs, to deter any of the wild beasts beyond the gate from escaping to ravage the people of London. Planks of wood, whitewashed and decorated with black scrawling words, hung from loops of rope tied to the fence. They read:

EXOTIC! MYSTERY! MONSTER!

NEW FROM THE DARKEST WILDS!

THE BEAST: NEVER BEFORE SPIED BY HUMAN EYES!

The aggressive letters jolted Lord Bart from his

erotic reverie. What could the zoo's newest addition be?

He approached the boy holding down the ticket booth. He was a short urchin with leering eyes beneath a jaunty newsboy cap. The sleeves of his tweed coat were stained dark from wiping his snotty nose.

"Two pounds, Sir," he said.

Lord Bart flashed his gold embossed invitation, tucked into his jacket pocket by the impeccable Aragon.

"Of course, Sir," said the urchin, unmoved from his position blocking Lord Bart's advancement.

He sighed and dug a fifty pence tip from a jingle of forgotten coin in the right pocket of his velvet coat. "Here you go, off with you."

The urchin shuffled aside. Lord Bart strode onwards.

Capuchin monkeys with cream faces and shoulders, contrasting with their black bodies, clung to spindly trees and hooted at him from the Monkey House. Golden lion tamarin watched him with shiny black eyes, looking so much like smaller, more agile versions of the desert cats.

Lord Bart strolled past yawning hippopotamus, shrieking white-feathered cockatiels, and a sad brown bear who plunked on his bottom and stared down at his belly without paying the slightest attention to any of his observers.

A stream of whispering people ignored all of these wonders, however; they flowed instead towards the centre of the zoo - the position of honour for the new exhibit.

Jungle flora sprang up from either side of the cement walkway. The atmosphere emerging before him grew tropical. A rumble shivered through the ground, stroking the soles of his feet through his Portuguese-cobbled oxfords. He quickened his step, heart beginning to thud.

A wide crowd spanned the width of the new enclosure.

London's ladies and gentry jostled each other for better vantage points, as usual. The rumble, again, lit through the concrete and tickled Lord Bart. Not a large man, he hovered behind a couple in tall, elaborate hats and strained to catch a glimpse of the new animal.

No - he would use his small stature to his advantage. He angled himself sideways and slipped between bodies, traversing the crowd with occasional pardons.

The unseen animal emitted heavy, deep breathing. Lord Bart squeezed his small, velvet self to the front of the crowd and gripped the fence, his chin level with the midway point of a fence with barbs topping each black rod.

They loomed from the crest of a small hill, that dipped down into an area feathered with ferns and leafy plants, ending in a wide moat.

The animal seemed at first to be a strange cross between lizard and turtle, enormous, with a flat back offering spikes and a long curved tail ending in a frilled club. Glossy black feathers decorated the club, like a Spanish dancer's alluring fan. The lizard took delicate nips from the crux of a fern, aware of the crowd, but powerful enough not to feel disturbed.

"Heaven's - what is that monster?" To Lord Bart's right, a woman covered her mouth with a white gloved hand and asked her husband.

"Have some decorum, dearest," said the husband, "that's no way to address a lady. The beast before you is a young, vibrant Ankylosaurus plucked at the height of her mating capabilities from the dark jungle of South America."

"My goodness," said the wife.

"Indeed," said the husband, "powerful, nubile, and without company. I pity her - she's likely very lonely."

Lady Ankylosaurus held her armoured body on thick, powerful legs. Her muscles pulsed as she shifted her bulk to address a new fern.

Lord Bart's pulse quickened. Was this the strong woman he had been searching for his entire life? The dinosaur swung her tail and the feathered fan shivered. Lord Bart felt that shiver work its way down to his groin.

Her snout silhouetted by the fern, the Ankylosaur raised her gaze to the crowd. A frond brushing each scaled cheek (were they scales? Or were they the softest, most delicate feathers? He wanted to know.) She locked eyes with Lord Bart.

His heart stopped for one moment, two. Was he dying? It beat again. He gasped.

Lady Ankylosaurus fluttered her lashes. Her eyes weren't black, as he initially thought -- they were the darkest tint of jade - an exotic, precious stone his father's shipping company imported from the

Far East. They waded through mutual gaze, moving deeper into the connection. Lord Bart felt her acknowledgement rise above his knees, his hips, and as it reached his chest his heart clenched, again. He murmured to her. Layers of frills rose from her throat and behind her eyes. The frills glowed peach. She purred.

A poem grew within him.

"Fair lady, feathered queen

Your aura - exotic, but serene

Fills me with longing and fire

New and formidable desires

Smothered only by your strength

Atop me, crush me with the length

Of your body, sweet lady -

I long to caress you

Say yes, Ankylosaur Queen

Your servant waits to please."

He would prepare and return to her on the morrow, to serenade her, and thus court her dominance.

CHAPTER THREE

"NEVER BEFORE SPIED BY HUMAN EYES."

HUMAN EYES, indeed, thought Lord Bart as he sat in his carriage the following day, giddy and nearly sick with anticipation. Her eyes *had* seemed almost human; certainly, they were full of a dark intelligence. This was no beast. This was a woman, deserving of respect. Deserving of love.

That, he could grant her.

But how? And would she accept it? Or would she toss him aside to crumple like a silk handkerchief against the stone?

"We have arrived, milord," called the coachman from the front. Now was the time.

"Back again so soon?" smirked the boy at the ticket booth. "It seems you enjoyed the display."

"It was sufficient for my purposes," sniffed Lord Bart, attempting to hide his excitement. Decades of stiff-upper-lip upbringing brought themselves to bear. "I simply thought to take some fresh air, and the London Zoo is as good a place as any."

"Most certainly," said the boy with a bow and a wink. "Two pounds, please."

Lord Bart tossed him two pounds sterling and stepped past the booth. He headed directly for Lady Ankylosaurus' enclosure, his heart pounding with each footstep, a blush staining his pale and delicate cheeks.

She reclined, regally, among a copse of ferns that swayed languorously in the slight river breeze. Her eyes were half-lidded. She seemed to be ignoring the crowd that chittered at the gates of the enclosure, as if they were beneath her notice, too rude and dumb for her queenly regard.

They *were*, of course. These sweating masses, slack-jowled and gammon-faced, were rightly beneath the notice of such a beast as this. *Not beast*, he thought. *A woman such as this.*

"My queen," he called out.

There was a small muttering in the crowd, and one large jolly man yelled, "Best you don't allow the king to hear you speak in such a way!"

Lord Bart fixed the man with an icy stare. "I suggest you keep to your own business," he said. The man shrugged and turned away, clearly preferring not to engage. Was it because he felt sorry for Lord Bart? Did he think he was weak?

He would make clear to these people - to everyone - that he was worthy of such a queen as this.

Meanwhile, Lady Ankylosaur had begun to stir. She rose from her bed of ferns and, to delighted gasps from the crowd, took a step forward on her powerful saurian legs.

Could it be that the earth itself shook slightly when her foot touched the ground?

The air was electric with anticipation. Lord Bart held his breath, involuntarily. The creature lumbered slowly towards him. Her eyes were jade pools, green as the ocean on a summer morning, green as the gardens he had played in as a child. They were depthless and yearning.

She approached him, never breaking eye contact, until she was close enough to touch.

"Fair lady," he whispered to her. "Feathered queen
- "

She exhaled, her warm breath brushing his hand.

Blood rushed to his face, and to other parts of him.
And he began to climb...

Mile High Pterodactyl Club

The heavy screeches overhead sent a pulse of excitement through Erin's body. She pushed back a heavy branch and pulled out a binocular, aiming the lens at the sky.

Her heart raced wildly when she caught a glimpse of one of them. The more she stared at it gliding through the clouds, the hotter she became. She was already so taken by the sight that she had no idea when she moved her hand over her chest, brushing her fingers over her hardened nipples.

Grinning, she put down the binoculars and squinted. There it was, its heavy wings beating majestically.

"So close," she muttered to herself and trudged forward, slicing through blades of grass, each minute taking her closer to her target. This was going to be one of the best experiences ever, better than all her other sexy time-travel adventures.

If only she could get close enough.

Erin followed the screeching sounds and went deeper into the jungle. The earth trembled around her as a loud roar echoed in the distance.

"A giganotosaurus," she muttered to herself, a soft chuckle escaping her lips. She tapped a watch-like device on her wrist, securing herself in a force field. Nothing could harm her now.

She hastened her steps, running through the thick brush. Her eyes went up to the sky and she saw it again—the reason she'd traveled back in time to this prehistoric era. The ground elevated as she ran, and she soon found herself ascending up a mountain.

"Okay, this is crazy," she panted. "You're going to lose them!"

The screeches grew quieter as the creatures flew farther away.

With a frantic push of a button on the device on her wrist, the space before her ripped apart and she stepped through, teleporting herself straight to the peak of the mountain.

She felt her body stretching and thinning as she warped through space, and then a splash of light hit her face when she burst out above the mountain. Perfect, she thought for a second. Except she'd somehow overshot it and found herself free falling through the sky.

Sharp winds slapped against her face as she tried to reach for her teleportation device.

Suddenly, a heavy screech echoed around her and a pterodactyl swooped in from underneath her. She clung to it, her heart beating fast, and slowly opened her eyes.

This is happening, she thought, embracing the creature tightly. The warmth of its body spread through to hers as she clung to it, and it let out a deep groan.

"Thank you," Erin whispered to it, stroking the back of its neck with the tip of her fingers. It let out soft sounds and she smiled. "You're enjoying this, aren't you?" she asked in a soft, sensual tone.

The pterodactyl responded with a slight shake, and more groans. Erin bit her lips and carefully straddled the creature while in mid-flight. This was an experience she'd always wanted to try and somehow, she'd fallen straight into it.

The humans from the future had discovered that dinosaurs were more intelligent and sensual than previously thought. Now, it was a wild experience daredevils like her sought out: deep sexual encounters with dinosaurs.

Erin was certain no one had experienced such with a pterodactyl before.

The pterodactyl couldn't speak, but she knew it could understand her, feel her touches and respond to them.

It flew higher into the clouds, giving Erin a view of the splash of colors below.

"It feels like it's just us up here," she whispered. She felt her shorts riding up her crotch as she clasped her thighs together, adjusting herself on top of its back.

It let out a soft moan and glided steadily.

"Don't worry, I'm not afraid of falling," she said and moved upward, putting her arms around its long neck. The thrill only increases with more danger, she always told herself.

Erin placed her hand flat on its neck, feeling

the subtle pulse rushing through its body. She caressed gently, moaning softly, and smiled when it responded with a shiver and a slight moan.

The low sounds of pleasure increased as she caressed its neck, letting her know it was enjoying it. She kept going, unbothered by the wind against her face. She stretched her legs and flattened her body and pressed her huge breasts on its back, slowly writhing on top of the creature.

Her hands continued stroking and caressing, and her moans drifted around the creature's face. She shut her eyes and held tight to the pterodactyl, her body moving to its rhythm as it flew lower. She could feel the vibrations rushing through its body as they were locked in a sensual embrace; feel its pleasure mount and near eruption.

And at the same time, it sent waves of tingles through her body. They were wrapped as one in the moment, gliding the clouds, experiencing the height of pleasure.

An idea popped up in her head. She sat up and took off her top, letting her boobs bounce freely. Then, she carefully slid off her shorts.

Her nipples were harder than ever, and she was soaking wet between her legs. She stuffed her clothes in her backpack and embraced the pterodactyl, rubbing her bare body against its. It must have felt the difference because it moaned and shook its head, weaving through the sky.

Erin could barely stand when her feet finally touched the ground. She giggled and wrapped her arms around the pterodactyl again, once again teasing it by sliding her hand down its belly and stroking it. She loved the way it moaned and shivered when she touched it, and the way her body also heated up in response.

"We're going to have to do this again someday," she whispered and opened up a portal, ready to get off to her next sexy adventure.

I wonder who'll be the first to spot the naked time traveler with a backpack, she thought slyly.

Dino Love Tips

DINO LOVE TIP #423

When mounting a quadrupedal dino mate, it's best to use your rear haunches as both a structural system but also as a pivoting system. Remember: both force and pleasure come straight from the hips, but the knees are the gateway to fun.

DINO LOVE TIP #225

If your mate has large spikes protruding wildly from its tail, it's highly recommended to place tennis balls over the tip of each spike. This ensures that any wildly wanton tail flailing won't inadvertently skewer your genitals to your leg! Unless, of course, you're into that sort of thing! *wink*

DINO LOVE TIP #88

When attempting to attract your dino mate, it's certainly ideal to utilize your biological features as much as dinosaurily possible. Flare that frilled crest or waggle those horns, you sexy beast, you!

DINO LOVE TIP #13

So there is a prevalence of rough sexual play in your nesting colony? It's important to know the rules going in. Before embarking on any nest intrusion fantasy, make sure you discuss safe words in advance. Try not to make it something everyday like RAAWWWWGG. Instead choose something you wouldn't normally say at the moment like "Pineapple" or "Spatula".

DINO LOVE TIP #212

Try a sex game where you trade off. Elizabeth Wright, a licensed psychotherapist, sex therapist, and Triceratops, suggests "stop and start." You set a timer on your phone for four minutes, where you have that amount of time to do anything to your partner (ranging from small nibbling to goring with your horns). Once the time's up, you switch places and the giver becomes the receiver, and vice versa.

And now, a sneak peek of

The Elf and the Milf

the Storm Crow Press's next offering…

CHAPTER ONE

Holly needed *something.*

She was on her way to the gym, as she always did on a Monday morning after dropping the kids off at school. The other moms looked at her sideways, she knew, when she showed up for drop-off in tight yoga pants and a crop top: their tired eyes and messy buns contrasted with Holly's perfect winged eyeliner and pert bottom.

It wasn't her fault they didn't like her – what in the world was wrong with wanting to look good? She never judged them. She used to be just like them. But she'd started working out for her own edification, and now she couldn't stop. It made her feel strong and desirable.

It made her feel like someone worth looking at.

Not that her husband Bruce would think so. But she'd long since given up trying to impress him. No, this was more… outwardly oriented.

She didn't know what exactly she needed, but it was *something*. Her life was busy with the demands of a family and a house and her part-time job as an art photographer, and yet she had never been so bored. Something in her paced like a caged tiger.

She pulled her mini-SUV into a parking spot and headed into the gym, giving a friendly wave to the girl at the front desk. A few minutes in the locker room, a scrunchie in her thick auburn hair, and she was ready to go: she leapt up onto her favourite treadmill and was setting it for a 45-minute hill run when she looked up and saw him.

He shone. There was no other word for it.

His skin was golden; not tan, exactly, but truly golden, with a sheen that nearly defied physics. His eyes were the deepest green-brown of a shaded forest, his hair so darkly black that it seemed woven from the night sky itself.

"I think you dropped this," he said to her, holding out the towel that seemed to have slipped off her shoulders between the dressing room and the treadmill. She barely registered what he was saying, though. She couldn't stop looking at him.

Stop it, Holly. This isn't cute.

"Thanks," she said. Even his voice was smooth and beautiful, like his skin.

What she could see, that was. She wondered if the rest of him was that golden.

"Are you all right?"

"Oh, yes," Holly said. "I've never been better." This man was the most gorgeous she'd ever seen, sure, but she went to the gym, too. She knew how her breasts looked in that sports bra, and how her short-shorts emphasized her lean thighs. She knew that the gym lighting was kind to her abs.

She'd worked hard for this body. Maybe now it would start working hard for her. She imagined how it would look nestled next to this golden man, skin to skin, limbs entangled…

"Have I seen you here before?"

"I just moved here," he said. "I'm from way up north. This is day one in the big city."

"And the first thing you did was go to the gym."

"Well," he said with a flash of brilliant smile, "fitness is important to me. It looks like it's important to you, too."

Heat rose in Holly's cheeks. He was flirting. He stepped closer, and she could smell his scent, a freshness of air like a clearing in the woods on a sunny day. His face was even more handsome up close: a classic jaw, long straight nose, wide deep-set eyes, and ears that... came to a point? How strange.

"I do enjoy exertion," she said with a wry smile of her own. "All kinds."

"It sounds like we have something in common, then."

They gazed at each other. Holly's heart began to race in a way that she had never experienced.

Not even with Bruce? No – he'd been a safe choice. A good, if bland, father. A dutiful, if uninspired and inconsistent, lover. At least at first.

Really, if she was honest with herself, he'd been the checkbox labeled "Husband" on her list of things to accomplish by the time she was thirty. And now she was thirty-seven, at her sexual peak, and she hadn't had sex in nearly a year. She hadn't had *good* sex in probably half a decade.

The realization came upon her, suddenly as a summer storm: this was going to happen.

This was *happening.*

She pulled her hair loose and shook it out, dismounting from the treadmill. "You know," she said, "I think I'd prefer a different kind of exercise. Care to join me?"

He grinned.

"I would indeed."

COMING SOON FROM STORM CROW PRESS

- The Elf and the MILF
- Easy Being Green: A Multi-Orc-asmic Compendium
- Undead In Bed: A Zombie Sextacular
- I Vant To Suck Your Cock: Gay Vampires In Love
- The 300-Year-Old Virgin
- Boning the Skeleton
- Mummy Dearest

ABOUT THE AUTHOR

From an early age Lola Faust's fantasies and reveries tilted towards the baroque, the unusual, and the eccentric. Though she entertained curious private journals, it wasn't until she entered the Paleontology program at the University of British Columbia that her fantastic and romantic notions concerning dinosaurs took full flight.

While working towards her doctorate, Ms Faust began writing her signature saurian prose. Today she is employed by day at a leading university in her field, but maintains her anonymous and risque personality online.

To learn more about the author and their other works, visit *lolafaust.com*

Printed in Great Britain
by Amazon

d06cd0da-5efd-483d-a349-697296801023R01